JORGE LUIS BORGES

FICCIONES

Jorge Luis Borges was one of those very rare creators who changed the face of an art form – in his case, the short story. His work has been paid the ultimate honor of being appropriated and imitated by innumerable writers on every continent of the world. But the true measure of his greatness lies in the fact that his fictions – elaborately paradoxical, post-modern, and intellectually delicious as they are – managed to return the short story to the realm of the fabulous and the uncanny from which, as parable and fairy tale, it originally came.

EVERYMAN,
I WILL GO WITH THEE,
AND BE THY GUIDE,
IN THY MOST NEED
TO GO BY THY SIDE

JORGE LUIS BORGES

Ficciones

with an Introduction by
John Sturrock

EVERYMAN'S LIBRARY

Alfred A. Knopf New York Toronto

166

THIS IS A BORZOI BOOK

PUBLISHED BY ALFRED A. KNOPF, INC.

First included in Everyman's Library, 1993
Copyright © 1962 by Grove Press, Inc., New York
Translated from the Spanish © 1956 by Emecé Editores S. A.,
Buenos Aires
This edition published in arrangement with Grove Press
Fourth printing

Introduction, Bibliography and Chronology Copyright © 1993 by
David Campbell Publishers Ltd.
Typography by Peter B. Willberg

ISBN 0-679-42299-4
LC 92-55353

Library of Congress Cataloging-in-Publication Data
Borges, Jorge Luis, 1899–1986
[Ficciones. English]
Fictions / Jorge Luis Borges.
p.   cm.—(Everyman's library)
ISBN 0-679-42299-4
I. Title.
PQ7797.B635F513   1993   92-55353
863—dc20   CIP

Book Design by Barbara de Wilde and Carol Devine Carson

Typeset in the UK by MS Filmsetting Limited, Frome, Somerset

Printed and bound in Germany
by Graphischer Grossbetrieb Pössneck GmbH

FICCIONES

CONTENTS

——

INTRODUCTION

Like his native continent, Jorge Luis Borges was slow to experience 'discovery' from Europe. At the age of sixty and with his life's writing three parts done, he was hardly more than a local writer, an Argentinian known if at all only to the more inquisitive followers of Spanish, and a choice few French readers who had come across him in translation. But by seventy Borges was one of the most published, most referred to and most lionized of living writers, a private man elevated late in life into an unforeseen celebrity. The translation into French of the *Ficciones* was the start of it: because, in his own words, 'until I appeared in French I was practically invisible – not only abroad but at home in Buenos Aires'. But the great thing was that in 1961 he won a half-share (the other half went to Samuel Beckett) of a literary prize, the Prix Formentor, a fashionable if short-lived award which this one time had the happy effect of moving a wonderfully good but shy and hitherto provincial writer into full international view. With this, Borges at last entered in his own person into the European literary world that he had inhabited hypothetically since he was a boy, first as a reader and then as a writer who, by the depth and sharpness of his literary intelligence, had far outgrown the literary community of Buenos Aires. In no time at all, he, or at any rate his finest single work, the *Ficciones*, was in English; the translations which reappear in the present edition were first published in 1962.

It is sometimes hard to remember that Borges didn't himself write these epochal stories straight into English, in which they read as to the language born. But then writing as transparent, as cool, as geometrical as this travels well between languages, with reassuringly little of that sacrifice of body and nuance sometimes held to define rather than simply qualify the act of translation. Where literature was concerned, English was always the language in which Borges was the most knowledgeably and comfortably at home. There had from the start been Englishness in his family, in people as well as books. A grandmother who had come out from England in the 1860s lived on to a great age and was a focal presence in his early home life, as a source of stories not least – her maiden name, Haslam, and her county of origin, Staffordshire, have both been discreetly inserted by Borges into the text of these *Ficciones*, as secret tokens of a familial piety that he never lost. Another name one might have hoped to find him dropping there is that of his English nanny, Miss Tink, memorable in her own right but also for having had a cousin John who went to the bad and became a 'hoodlum' in Buenos Aires, in something like a mirror-image of the passage from a rough culture to a smooth which Borges himself was to follow as he grew up into a writer. But no Tinks have been given asylum in these pages.

An English granny, an English nanny, and two parents who both of them knew English and both read in it: it isn't surprising that this should have been the language in which Borges first learnt to read and which all through his life meant the most to him, to the point where, approaching his sixties, having become a professor of English and American literature at the university in Buenos Aires, he took up English in its earliest form, of Anglo-Saxon, and taught it to his students there, being so charmed by its alien northern sounds that, polite and reticent man though he habitually was, he admits to having joined with his class in shouting out Old English sentences on their way down the city streets.

But Borges was a man of several foreign languages, not of English alone. As a reader he grew up polyglot, coming to know French, German and Italian, the Italian of Dante and Ariosto, not of the vaguely criminal Buenos Aires district of Palermo, first settled by Sicilians, in which he spent his boyhood. What Borges wanted from languages was their literature and in the reading he did he was already the honorary European, acting out from the start the belief he later expressed that, for educated Argentinians like himself, 'our tradition is the whole of western culture, and ... we have a better right to that tradition than the inhabitants of any one particular western nation can have'. The thinness of the local literary tradition, which went back less than a century, meant that Argentinians should look abroad, and first and foremost to those western European cultures which had fed over the years into the Argentinian. And how perceptively and assiduously Borges himself did his looking, on his way to becoming the fluent synthesist of a great range of foreign writing and thought.

And here history stepped in to help him, because for seven years the Borges family was more or less trapped in Europe, having gone there on a visit in the unlucky year of 1914. A visit became residence once World War I had broken out. (It had been planned partly so that Borges' father could get treatment for the serious congenital eye trouble he suffered from, which couldn't be cured and which he passed on to his son; both in the end went blind.) From 1914 to 1918 Borges was ideally placed to enrich further the linguistic mix to which his parents' own cosmopolitan tastes had already introduced him: he was at school in Geneva – the international city he was seventy years later, with some appropriateness, to die in, on a return visit, at the age of eighty-six. From Geneva he went to Lugano and then for two years to Spain. By now he had tried writing in English – 'Wordsworthian sonnets' – and in French; among Spanish-speakers in Majorca and Seville he resumed the use of that language, though there was now even less danger that he would shrink once back in South America into an isolationist writer, forgetful of all that was to be gained from the endlessly various literatures of western Europe.

In the years in which he was still able to read, before his sight failed him, Borges read more and in greater detail in English than in any of the other languages he knew, Spanish included. And because reading and writing soon went closely together for him, he also wrote copiously about English (and some North American) authors in the many essays he published in Argentinian reviews and periodicals. What drew him was, first the congenial ideas and odd erudition that he found in them and in the second place technique, those too easily overlooked formalities by which writers get their effects, in prose as well as verse. Borges read with the head, not with his feelings. If he admires Keats' 'Ode to a Nightingale', this isn't because he finds that poem especially moving or beautiful but because he relishes the philosophical idea on which it turns, of all nightingales being in effect one bird and thereby immortal, as indistinguishable realizations of a single Platonic Form. And so it is in general with Borges' reading; he is looking to supply his mind, repeatedly going back to curious ideas that other readers might have little time for, such as Coleridge's fancy of waking up from a floral dream holding in his hand a real flower – for Borges an allegory of the creative process itself, which in taking thought adds real objects to the world: printed words.

English literature had a big part to play in the literary ascesis through which Borges put himself in the 1920s. Once he had returned home to Argentina with his family and had begun seriously to write, the poems and essays that he produced were very unlike what he came to write later. His first manner was still under the influence of the so-called Ultraism he had met with in Spain, the local version, and a mainly very feeble one, of Expressionism. This youthful Borges was by his own account over-loud, Romantic, bent on surprising if not shocking his readers by the violence of his imagery. He wrote essays whose aim, he later confessed, 'was to be bitter and relentless', and a collection of poems in an overheated free verse which celebrated the Bolshevik Revolution of 1917. Neither essays nor poems were ever published because he eventually destroyed them, so far were they from being the work of the imperturbable writer who was to be known as Jorge Luis Borges. But over these ten years or so Borges gradually became Borges, as his excitement cooled and he learnt the self-effacing ways of the classicist, writing prose where before he had written mainly poetry and purging his style of anything too crudely emotive or sensational.

The seventeen stories of *Ficciones* were first collected and published in the early 1940s. It helps when reading them to know that Borges didn't always write as sparely or objectively as he does here, that he is a reformed lyricist, because the evolution he had passed through as a young writer remained as an important part of his subject-matter in his maturity. He was fond of referring back to it, so that people should know how far and from where as a writer he had come. Writing, in

1969, a new preface to a book of poems with what by now had become for him the shamingly upbeat title of *Fervor de Buenos Aires*, first published in 1923, Borges summed up the progress he had made since that fervent time with the <u>wry brevity</u> of which he was a master: 'In those days, I sought dusk, the outskirts, and unhappiness; now, mornings, the centre and serenity.'

Contained in these few words is a reminder that as he distanced himself fastidiously from his own first callow efforts in literature, Borges distanced himself at the same time from the indigenous but undeveloped literature of Argentina. This was a literature which he knew well, which he wrote about understandingly though with a critical reserve that the cultural chauvinists in Buenos Aires didn't like him for, and which eventually became for him a source of themes to be transposed ironically in his stories, as here in the stories called 'The End' and 'The South'. The word 'outskirts' in the preface I have just quoted from is a clue to the nature of that irony. It was in the *arrabales*, the outskirts of Buenos Aires, that he had spent his boyhood, and there that he had first come to sense that culturally at least he did not belong fully in the country of his birth. The first book of prose that he published, in 1930, was a short study of a neighbour in Palermo who was also a minor and very typical Argentinian poet, Evaristo Carriego, a louche character and a sentimental writer towards whom Borges shows great fairness in discriminating between what was false and what was good in his poetry. But he uses this essay more than anything to demonstrate where he stands himself in respect of the cultural inheritance of such as Carriego, which was not worthless but was by Borges' standards elementary and naive. Similarly, the reckless machismo of a Carriego was not a way of life likely to appeal to the courteous and bookish Borges, except as a literary motif. By 1930 he knew where he stood in this respect; he begins the preface to the Carriego book: 'For years I believed I had grown up in a suburb of Buenos Aires, a suburb of risky streets and visible sunsets. The truth is I grew up in a garden, behind lanceolate railings, and in a library of unlimited English books.'

FICCIONES

This is concisely put as ever, and an antithesis more highly charged than it might appear, holding as it does the key to the dialectical process on which Borges' whole literary career turned. First had come the years in which he wrote in the faulty belief that he might himself be an Evaristo Carriego, the laureate of the 'risky streets and visible sunsets', a realist that is, versifying the gaudy materiality of the world around him. But after a number of years spent in pursuit of this mistaken vocation, Borges had seen the light. He was no Carriego, no street-poet, born to live dangerously, but a timid, short-sighted, middle-class lover of books, born safely into the bourgeoisie even if he had lived as a boy in a rather dubious part of town. But this mild experience of alienation could be used to his advantage, because it meant that he had once been in close proximity to that cultural Other against which he would go on measuring himself, with an increasing irony as he aged and as the odd notion that he might once have become a true denizen of the *arrabales* seemed more and more far-fetched.

The 'reality' of Evaristo Carriego and his kind thus became a crucial part of Borges' literary mythology. There is both an urban and a rural side to it. The rural side is the better known, outside Argentina, because it centres on the archetypal figure of the *gaucho* or cattleman, who along with the tango may count as the most distinctive of Argentina's cultural exports to the twentieth century. The urban side we know next to nothing about, but the street equivalent of the *gaucho* for Borges is the *compadrito*, the petty gangster or hoodlum, like John Tink or Carriego himself, who were quite often caught up in the endemic corruption and violence of local politics. The *gaucho* and the *compadrito* share something positive: a huge self-reliance and what Borges somewhere calls 'the religion of friendship', the true religion, he thought, of an only nominally Catholic country. They also share something more un-pleasant: a promptness to resor' to the knife in settling their differences.

Gauchos, hoodlums, and above all the knife-fighters, not forgetting the guitar music that is the rightful accompaniment to native themes such as these, frequently find their way into

xvi

INTRODUCTION

Borges' stories, the later collections especially, those he published in his seventies. But they are only ever blatant figments,
never introduced for the sake of a naive realism or, perish the
thought, local colour. There is nothing so simple as local
colour in Borges and to read him as if there were is to misread
him grievously. He grew up, we should remember, 'in a
garden, and behind lanceolate railings, and in a library of
unlimited English books'. Reality came to him mediated
through books, its tedium and occasional threats displaced by
the enjoyable phantasms of the writer. The garden and, rather
more obviously, the library are sites of ultimate pleasure for
this resolute and gifted escapist and both have a story
accorded them in *Ficciones*, 'The Garden of Forking Paths' in
the one case, 'The Library of Babel' in the other.

The first of these stories, one of the most alarmingly
ingenious Borges ever wrote, may seem on the face of it to have
little to do with gardens, although it contains one. But the
fantastic story itself, like the fantastic story it is about, is meant
to be enjoyed as if it were a garden, a *locus amoenus*, a secluded
and untroubled place in which the maker of the story has
taken his pleasure and where his readers can now do the same,
striving as best they can to trace the hidden logic of a hugely
complicated, not to say labyrinthine narrative. As for 'The
Library of Babel', that is a story sufficiently cheerless on the
surface to suggest that Borges found libraries detestable or
fearsome rather than agreeable places. The library of Babel is
either infinite in size or so incalculably vast as to be as good (or
as bad) as infinite. It has its nightmarish aspects and it's true
that Borges had some reason to dislike libraries because for
nine years 'of solid unhappiness', from 1937 to 1946, he was
obliged to work in one, as a quite junior librarian, in order to
make money. The cataloguing work he did was futile but
never hard and it was during these same years that he wrote,
partly in office hours, his finest stories, those collected in
Ficciones and *The Aleph*. (He finally lost this job when he was
'promoted' by the populist Perón regime (of which he had
been an outspoken critic) to the 'inspectorship of poultry and
rabbits in the public markets', a slight which led to him being
invited by the new regime to become Director of the National

Library of Argentina after Perón fell.) There are no doubt one or two sardonic echoes of his bad experiences in his first library job in 'The Library of Babel' but in principle if not necessarily in fact libraries were good places for Borges and the point of his story lies elsewhere. It is in fact a typically vertiginous speculation that starts out from the banal, one might have thought harmless truth that language as we know it works by combining a quite small number of fixed elements first into words and then into sentences. 'The Library of Babel' pursues the possibilities of this fact to a most uncomfortable extreme: it is the bad dream of a Structuralist, not of a bored Buenos Aires librarian.

There is one other item in the décor of Borges' suburban childhood which should not be taken at face value: the 'lanceolate railings' that marked the family garden off from the hazardous townscape beyond. Something to be remembered when reading Borges, even in the casual context of a preface, is that he uses so few words that all of them must be attended to. No writer has ever been more teasingly succinct. The lance-head railings could seem innocent enough, a quick dab of realism; surely there *were* such railings round the garden in Palermo? Perhaps so, but the brute fact of their existence will not do to explain why Borges has invoked them. 'It's possible, but not interesting', as the brilliant detective says to the dumb policeman in the story of 'Death and the Compass', thereby indicating the vital difference Borges wants us to recognize between fact and fiction, or what is given by the world and what is made by the writer. A Borgesian fiction is very much made and 'interesting' for having been so; it is a mystery demanding to be cleared up by those who read it.

Borges' lance-head railings may be read as something both given and made, both a memory and a metaphor – a point in the real world where fact and imagination converge. As a metaphor they point to a strain in Borges' ancestry which provides him with another of his local themes: the military strain. Some among his forbears in Argentina had been fighting men, and had died gallantly in action, in one or other of the civil wars or eruptions that punctuated Argentinian history after it won independence from Spain early in the nineteenth century. Borges salutes these warrior figures but without glorifying them; rather, he uses them further to define his own eirenic role as a man far removed from any need or capability even of displaying a physical bravery such as theirs. (The eirenic man no longer *does*, he *remembers* the deeds of others: Ireneo is the peaceable first name of Borges' unfortunate prodigy of memory, 'Funes the Memorious'.) His paternal grandfather, Colonel Francisco Borges, the husband found in Argentina by Fanny Haslam from Staffordshire, was killed in a skirmish in 1874. Recalling that death in his 'Autobiographical Essay', Borges reflects on the fact that the colonel had been shot dead by two bullets fired from a Remington rifle, and goes on a mite callously: 'This was the first time Remington rifles were used in the Argentine, and it tickles my fancy to think that the firm that shaves me every morning bears the same name as the one that killed my grandfather.' The thought is one to appeal to Vladimir Nabokov, another stylish devotee of the ironic coincidence. But between the Remington rifle and the Remington razor, there stretches for Borges the distance separating adventures of the body from those of the mind, the brutality of combat from the ease of domesticity, the untamed Argentina from his own civilized one. The only 'lances' Colonel Borges' genteel grandson will ever face are those on top of the railings round a Palermo garden.

All the more reason then why the writer of fiction should have played self-mocking games with the motif of physical bravery or heroism. A story after all needs a hero, so where better for someone who is by his nature less than heroic to promote himself into the fictive aristocracy of the valiant? The last story in the present collection, 'South', enacts just such a promotion. 'Perhaps my best story', Borges calls this, which isn't an opinion we have to share but is I think an indication that this story is autobiographical to an extent none of the others in *Ficciones* is. It shares an incident with the author's own life to which he ascribed great significance as having been instrumental in making him into a writer of fictions. The incident is that in which the story's hero, Juan Dahlmann, hits his head against a freshly painted door as he hurries upstairs,

FICCIONES

eager to examine 'an imperfect copy of Weil's edition of *The Thousand and One Nights*'. (The 'imperfect copy' of one of Borges' favourite books is a hint of narrative duplicities to come.) Dahlmann's wound seems slight but it becomes infected, and he nearly dies of septicemia. This illness with its attendant fever is the cardinal moment of an exceedingly subtle story, the second part of which re-enacts the first in an opposite, this time heroic register.

The entire episode repeats one that Borges recounts elsewhere as fact, it having happened to him on Christmas Eve of 1938, when, also running upstairs, he hit his head against, not a freshly painted door but a freshly painted casement window, and received a flesh wound that also led to a life-threatening septicemia. In his convalescence from this illness, fearful that his intellectual powers had been permanently weakened or even wrecked by the fits of delirium he had been through, he thought to test them by writing something of a kind he had not attempted before: 'I decided I would try to write a story. The result was "Pierre Menard, Author of *Don Quixote*".' That story is here, in *Ficciones*; it is perhaps the most quoted of all Borges' stories, an engaging satire but at the same time a very radical exercise in what we would nowadays want to call literary theory. The convalescent mind that could think up something as original, profound and at the same time amusing as this was certainly intact, *very* intact I would be inclined to say.

In one way, Borges' account of how he came to write 'Pierre Menard' is misleading: this was not the first story he had written, even if it was more ambitious than anything he had done earlier. One story which predated it appears in *Ficciones*, 'The Approach to Al-Mu'tasim', which takes the very Borgesian form of the review of a non-existent novel, true to his dictum that the most economical way to 'postulate' a complex reality is to describe it not in itself but in a chosen few of its effects. Before this story, he had also published something called 'Streetcorner Man', an exercise in local colour written in a corrupt colloquial Spanish appropriate to its Argentinian theme of violence and revenge. More typically, Borges had published in 1935 a volume with the encyclopedic title of *A*

INTRODUCTION

Universal History of Infamy. This contains stories of infamous doings set in England, the United States, Japan, and the China Seas. They are not, however, Borges' stories, or only partly so, because they are stories found in other books and retold by him with alterations silently made to suit his needs. There may be a quiet joke going on here, inasmuch as Borges knew that the literary simpletons would look on his plagiarisms as themselves coming close to infamy, given that writers are commonly expected to invent the stories they tell and not steal them.

But Borges would say that that is an altogether wrong expectation. His own infamous procedure was in his eyes, as it should be in our own, an exemplary demonstration of the way in which new writing emerges not immediately from the real world but having made a detour through the writing which exists already. New stories are, inescapably, old stories with a difference – though this is *not* a judgement anyone will be able to apply to the stories in *Ficciones,* which are stories about stories and as such without precedent! The already written is to the writer a principal part of the real world, a given. There is no forgetting with Borges that although we may wishfully think of books as if they were immaterial reflections of the real, they are themselves material, additions to the forms of matter, just as that most privileged item of domestic furniture for Borges, the mirror, is a solid even though it exists in order to reflect. This idea and its implications are at the heart of the mysterious first story of *Ficciones,* 'Tlön, Uqbar, Orbis Tertius'.

A Universal History of Infamy may seem a presumptuous title for what is a slim book, containing a bare handful of stories of infamy, far-flung geographically it may be but hardly exhaustive of their theme. But the claim to universality is serious up to a point, because it bears out a principal axiom of Borges' philosophy as a writer: that language is by its abstract nature almost laughably reductive of the reality we use it to represent. We have rather few words by which to represent an inordinately varied reality. Take the noun 'universe' itself: a single term which we use to refer to an inconceivably plural and complex Universe. It might well seem inadequate to its referent. The realization of this inadequacy of language is

FICCIONES

never far away in Borges, who, writer of few words that he is,
delights in knowing that these few may stand as the ultimate
abstraction from real life, a verbal microcosm as it were,
seeming to contain multitudes. For all the world's infamy to be
rendered down to a hundred and fifty pages of Spanish prose is
thus simply a caustic acknowledgement on his part that
rendering down is what language specifically does, and that
the nutshell is in truth no mean container.

The few stories which Borges includes in his 'universal'
history are offered as archetypes therefore, which is one reason
why he feels free to take them over from other men's books,
because archetypes belong to no one. His own role in this is
archetypal also, as someone who receives a story, alters it, and
then passes it on, his contribution made as a temporary
leaseholder to the more or less anonymous traffic in narrative.
More or less but not entirely anonymous, for it is by his
alterations that the leaseholder is able to make his own name.
Modest he may be in respect of his sources, but Borges knows
he has the power too to intervene in literary history: 'Since the
general plots or circumstances were all given me, I had only to
embroider sets of vivid variations.' Changing the stories he has
been given makes them the more personal for him and the
more attractive to us; we would far rather read Borges'
versions than the now obsolete originals. And when it comes to
'vivid variations' it might be thought that no variation from
an original was ever so vivid as that attempted by the dogged
French littérateur Pierre Menard, whose manic ambition it is
to reproduce the original text of *Don Quixote* word for word.
Anyone who doubts that a textual clone such as this can rank
as a 'variation' should read Borges' delightful story and find
out how wrong they are.

The stories in *Ficciones* are the very best of Borges: they are
not, it should by this time be clear, for the intellectually inert
or the literal minded, because they mean more than they seem
to mean, having to do with literary and philosophical ideas
and not just with peculiar sequences of unreal events. Rather
than stories, they might best be read as essays for which he has
found a compelling and memorable narrative form. They are
short because everything Borges ever wrote was short, he

xxii

didn't believe in length. He claimed he had the greatest difficulty getting to the end of a novel in the days when he read them and seems never even to have been tempted to write a novel himself. Reading these *Ficciones*, it's easy to see why: they are both too compacted and too rigorous in their construction to be sustainable over many pages – and the complications of a whole novel by Borges written to these specifications don't bear thinking of.

Borges' fictions are narrative at its purest; they contain no psychology. His 'characters' are really no more than proper names or the embodiment of an idea, without an inner life to call their own. Intellection, not empathy, is what one is asked to bring to them, because there is no mistaking these artful figments for flesh and blood. No one should start feeling sorry for Funes the Memorious, the bedridden young man who is unable to forget anything he has ever experienced. Funes is an unfortunate right enough, but of no everyday kind: his inability to forget means he will never be a writer because he lacks that vital power of abstraction conferred by language; his memories in their disastrous completeness must remain forever as particulars, he can't even start to classify them. Is it any wonder that he should die in the end of a 'congestion'?

Borges would have hated in later life to be called a Modernist, let alone a Post-Modernist, a category of writer he didn't live to see. But he is post-modern in one sense at least: he is unfailingly aware that we use words to 'represent' a reality that is not very much of it verbal. Between language and the universe evoked by it there is a void, terrible if you take a tragic view of things, liberating if you are like Borges an ironist, since that void is also the condition of our freedom to use language as we will, to create fictions as well as register facts. There are times when Borges seems to be saying that all verbal constructs are fictive, that the surest way with language is to play intellectual games with it, as he does. He was as a man an extreme sceptic or agnostic, disbelieving of the truth claims of philosophers and even more of theologians, but fascinated all the same by some of the metaphysical notions they had over the centuries dreamt up, unconstrained as theology peculiarly is by objective evidence. He dwells lovingly on strange theologies such as that of the Gnostics, seeing them precisely as waking dreams, equivalent on a grander scale to his own fictions.

Borges' stories have been taken before now as serious essays in metaphysics and he himself as a committed metaphysician; but he was committed to play rather than to philosophy and his stories are the free speculations of someone quite widely read in metaphysics, eastern as well as western. For aesthetic reasons, Borges savours metaphysical ideas, but he sees no need to subscribe to them – except, that is, at those times when he is a practising writer of fiction. Then, he becomes a philosophical Idealist, or subscriber to the belief that reality is mental, that it is all in the mind as we say; as well as a Realist, in the medieval sense, or someone who believes that abstract terms have real existence, that 'redness', say, is a real entity, not simply an abstract quality common to all particular red things. The philosophers on whose authority Borges likes to draw are those who elaborated doctrines of this kind: Plato, Berkeley and Schopenhauer. He didn't for a moment believe that they had got things right, that Idealism was the final answer or that Realism was true. On the contrary, he knew that they were merely intriguing moments in the contradictory history of thought itself. But to the writer of fiction they could be something more than that. For in a fiction, 'reality' *is* purely mental, it doesn't exist beyond the words used to create it, and it is also the product of the fiction-maker's will: it simulates reality proper as understood in the philosophies of Berkeley and Schopenhauer. And because fictions are verbal and made of nothing but general terms, they subscribe also to the doctrine of Realism. These are the simple but provisional philosophical notions with which Borges went to work and which it is as well for the reader of Borges to keep in mind. To do so is to add to the pleasure of reading these unlikely and delectable *Ficciones*.

John Sturrock

SELECT BIBLIOGRAPHY

OTHER BOOKS BY BORGES TRANSLATED INTO ENGLISH
The Aleph and Other Stories, trans. Norman Thomas di Giovanni in collaboration with the author, 1970.
Doctor Brodie's Report, trans. Norman Thomas di Giovanni in collaboration with the author, 1971.
The Book of Sand, trans. Norman Thomas di Giovanni, 1977.
Dreamtigers (El Hacedor), trans. Mildred Boyer and Harold Morland, 1964.
A Universal History of Infamy, trans. Norman Thomas di Giovanni, 1972.
Other Inquisitions, trans. Ruth L. Simms, 1964.
Selected Poems, 1923–1967, ed. Norman Thomas di Giovanni, 1972.
The Gold of the Tigers: Selected later poems, trans. Alastair Reid, 1977.

BIOGRAPHY
Borges' own 'Autobiographical Essay' appears in the English translation of *The Aleph* listed above: an invaluable and entertaining source of information about his life.
EMIR RODRIGUEZ MONEGAL, *Jorge Luis Borges: A literary biography*, 1978. Written by a Uruguayan critic and Yale professor who knew Borges: long on intimate detail, short on analysis.

BOOKS ON BORGES IN ENGLISH
RICHARD BURGIN, *Conversations with Jorge Luis Borges*, 1968. Borges intelligently questioned and talking engagingly about his life and work.
EVELYN FISHBURN and PSICHE HUGHES, *A Dictionary of Borges*, 1990. Useful guide to the large number of authors, books, etc., alluded to in Borges' work.
D. L. SHAW, *Borges: Ficciones*, 1976. Short, sensible academic study.
—*Borges' Narrative Strategy*, 1992. Longer, more technical version of the study above.
JOHN STURROCK, *Paper Tigers: The ideal fictions of Jorge Luis Borges*, 1977. Borges' stories analysed as exercises in the theory of fiction.

CHRONOLOGY

DATE	AUTHOR'S LIFE	LITERARY CONTEXT
1899	August 24. Jorge Luis Borges born into the professional middle classes in Buenos Aires, to anglophone parents.	
1900		Conrad: *Lord Jim*. Freud: *The Interpretation of Dreams*.
1901	Birth of a younger sister, Norah.	James: *The Sacred Fount*. Mann: *Buddenbrooks*.
1902		Kipling: *Just So Stories*. William James: *Varieties of Religious Experience*. James: *The Wings of a Dove*.
1903		Butler: *The Way of All Flesh*.
1904		Conrad: *Nostromo*. Hudson: *Green Mansions*.
1905		Unamuno: *The Life of Don Quixote and Sancho*. Lugones: *La guerra gaucha* (The Gaucho War). Darío: *Songs of Life and Hope*. Wells: *Kipps*.
1905–6	First attempts at writing, imitations of Cervantes.	
1906		Conrad: *The Mirror of the Sea*.
1907		Conrad: *The Secret Agent*.
1908	A translation into Spanish of Oscar Wilde's 'The Happy Prince' published in a Buenos Aires newspaper.	Larreta: *The Glory of Don Ramiro*. Chesterton: *The Man Who Was Thursday*.
1909	First experience of the pampas, on a family visit to relatives living in the country north-west of Buenos Aires.	Lugones: *Lunario sentimental* (Sentimental Moon Calendar). Kipling: *Actions and Reactions*.
1910		
1911		Conrad: *Under Western Eyes*. Baroja: *The Tree of Science*.
1912		

HISTORICAL EVENTS

Boer War (to 1902).

Argentina signs boundary treaty with Chile. Founding of British Labour Party.

Chile and Argentina refer the question of boundaries to British arbitration. Death of Queen Victoria. Marconi transmits message across the Atlantic.

Wright Brothers' first successful powered flight.
Emmeline Pankhurst's militant 'suffragettes' in UK.

First Russian Revolution.

Death of Argentinian President, Manuel Quintana; José Figueroa Alcorta assumes Presidency.

Austria annexes Bosnia and Herzegovina.

First Model T Ford in US. Blériot flies across the Channel.

Argentina: Roque Sáenz Peña President. Death of Edward VII in UK. First Post-Impressionist exhibition held in London.
Zapata initiates guerrilla struggle in Mexico.

US Marines occupy Nicaragua (to 1925). Charlie Chaplin's first film.
Sinking of the *Titanic*.

DATE	AUTHOR'S LIFE	LITERARY CONTEXT
1913		Proust: *Swann's Way*.
		Lawrence: *Sons and Lovers*.
1914	Accompanies his parents to Europe and goes to school in Geneva.	Darío: *Song to Argentina and other poems*.
		Unamuno: *Mist*.
		Yeats: *Responsibilities*.
		Joyce: *Dubliners*.
1915	Visit to northern Italy, Venice and the Roman amphitheatre of Verona, in which he recites gaucho poetry.	Woolf: *The Voyage Out*.
		Ford: *The Good Soldier*.
		Lawrence: *The Rainbow*.
1916		Joyce: *A Portrait of the Artist as a Young Man*.
		Blasco Ibañez: *The Four Horsemen of the Apocalypse*.
1917		Eliot: *Prufrock and other Observations*.
1918	Family moves to spend a year in Lugano.	Hudson: *Far Away and Long Ago*.
		Spengler: *The Decline of the West*.
1919	Moves to Majorca, living in Palma and Valldemosa.	
1919–20	In Seville. First poem, a Walt Whitmanesque 'Hymn to the Sea', is published in a review belonging to a group called the Ultraists, who 'had set out to renew literature, a branch of the arts of which they knew nothing whatever'.	
1920	Moves to Madrid. Writes two books, one of essays, another of poems, both later destroyed.	Lawrence: *Women in Love*.
		Mansfield: *Bliss*.
1921	Returns to Buenos Aires, after an absence of seven years. Founding editor of *Prisma*, avant-garde review lasting two issues.	
1922	Helps to start and edit a second review, *Proa*, lasting for three issues.	Pirandello: *Henry IV*.
		Eliot: *The Waste Land*.
		Joyce: *Ulysses*.
		Mansfield: *The Garden Party*.
		Woolf: *Jacob's Room*.

CHRONOLOGY

Revolution in Mexico City. Second Balkan War.

US forces occupy Veracruz and Haiti (to 1934). Beginning of World War I (to 1918).

Mexico: Carranza is recognized as President of Mexico by US and eight Latin American states.

Argentina: In a secret ballot, Hipólito Irigoyen becomes President and initiates reforms in labour working conditions. Mexico: Francisco 'Pancho' Villa undertakes raids on US soil to embarrass Carranza. US sends 12,000 troops to pursue Villa.

Argentina: President Irigoyen maintains Argentina's strict neutrality in World War I despite pressure exerted by US President Woodrow Wilson. Mexico ratifies new Constitution. US Marines occupy Cuba (to 1923). Brazil declares war on Germany. Russian Revolution.

US Marines occupy Honduran ports. Increasingly authoritarian leadership in Peru. Zapata shot dead by troops in Mexico.

Argentina leaves the League of Nations in protest at the Allies' repressive policy to defeated Germany, re-joining in 1927. Carranza murdered by one of his own supporters in Mexico. Arturo Alessandri elected President in Chile.

Argentina: Radical Party returned at general election; Marcelo T. de Alvear elected President.

DATE	AUTHOR'S LIFE	LITERARY CONTEXT
1923	Publishes *Fervor de Buenos Aires*, a first book of poems. Meets Macedonio Fernández, an eccentric Argentinian writer and conversationalist, author of a novel with twenty chapters and fifty-six forewords.	Svevo: *The Confessions of Zeno.* Hemingway: *Three Stories and Ten Poems.*
1924	*Proa* relaunched and survives for fifteen issues.	Neruda: *Twenty Love Poems and a Song of Despair.* Pirandello: *Each in His Own Way.* Mann: *The Magic Mountain.* Breton: *Manifesto of Surrealism.* Azorín: *Una Hora de España.*
1925	Publishes *Luna de Enfrente*, a second collection of poems, 'a kind of riot of sham local colour'.	Ortego y Gasset: *The Dehumanization of Art.* Woolf: *Mrs Dalloway.* Fitzgerald: *The Great Gatsby.* Kafka: *The Trial.*
1926		Faulkner: *Soldier's Pay.* Kafka: *The Castle.* Lawrence: *The Plumed Serpent.* Guiraldes: *Don Segundo Sombra.*
1927		Lorca: *Canciones (1921–1924).* J. W. Dunne: *An Experiment with Time.* Woolf: *To the Lighthouse.* Cather: *Death Comes for the Archbishop.* Hemingway: *Men Without Women.* Hesse: *Steppenwolf.*
1928		Lawrence: *Lady Chatterley's Lover.* Bulgakov: *The Master and Margarita* (to 1940). Macedonio Fernández: *No todo es vigilia la de los ojos abiertos* (We're not always awake when our eyes are open).
1929	*Cuaderno San Martín*, a third book of poems, published. Wins a literary prize from the city of Buenos Aires for a collection of essays, since suppressed.	Lorca: *Gypsy Ballads.* Moravia: *The Time of Indifference.* Faulkner: *The Sound and the Fury.* Hemingway: *A Farewell to Arms.* Macedonio Fernández: *Papeles de Recienvenidos* (Newcomers' Papers). Ortega y Gasset: *The Rebellion of the Masses.*

CHRONOLOGY

Assassination of 'Pancho' Villa in Mexico. End of Ottoman Empire. Coolidge US President, Baldwin Prime Minister in UK.

US Marines land in Honduras. Rebellion in Brazil. Military junta in Chile. Mexico quarrels with US over oil rights legislation. Death of Lenin.

Chile: A 'young officers' coup removes the junta. Mussolini embarks on creation of Fascist state in Italy. Reconstitution of Nazi Party in Germany.

US Marines occupy Nicaragua and organize the National Guard. Rebellion by militant Catholics in Mexico. Germany admitted to League of Nations. General Strike in UK.

Chile: Carlos Ibañez assumes Presidency; his harsh regime survives till 1931. Lindbergh flies the Atlantic solo. German financial crisis.

Argentina: Hipólito Irigoyen returned as President; Radical Party in strong position to initiate social reform and industrialization. Mexico: General Alvaro Obregón re-elected President but is assassinated by a religious fanatic two weeks later. First Five Year Plan in USSR. Discovery of penicillin.

Mexico: Formation of National Revolutionary Party. Under several names this party institutionalizes the Mexican revolution into a bureaucratic apparatus. Chile/Peru: Following US arbitration, a long-standing territorial dispute is settled, Tacna becoming Peruvian and Arica Chilean. Trotsky banished from USSR. Hunger marches in UK. Collapse of the New York Stock Exchange.

FICCIONES

DATE	AUTHOR'S LIFE	LITERARY CONTEXT
1930	Publishes *Evaristo Carriego*, a study of 'a nearly invisible popular poet' who was also a friend of the Borges family.	Pirandello: *Tonight We Improvise*. Freud: *Civilization and its Discontents*. Musil: *The Man Without Qualities*. Auden: *Poems*. Eliot: *Ash Wednesday*.
1931		Wilson: *Axel's Castle*. Woolf: *The Waves*.
1932	*Discusión*, the earliest of Borges' essay collections to survive as part of his published *Obra completa*.	Faulkner: *Light in August*. Hemingway: *Death in the Afternoon*.
1933		Neruda: *Residence on Earth* (to 1935). Jung: *Modern Man in Search of a Soul*.
1934		Fitzgerald: *Tender is the Night*.
1935	*Historia universal de la infamia* (A Universal History of Infamy), a collection of stories first published in a Buenos Aires newspaper and consisting of 'free' versions of stories he had read elsewhere.	Eduardo Mallea: *Historia de una pasión argentina*.
1936	*Historia de la eternidad* (History of Eternity), essays chiefly to do with metaphysical ideas concerning the nature of Time. Translates Virginia Woolf's *Orlando*, followed by *A Room of One's Own*.	Eliot: *Collected Poems*. Faulkner: *Absalom, Absalom!*. Nabokov: *Despair*.
1937	Forced to take a job in a Buenos Aires public library.	Silone: *Bread and Wine*. Hemingway: *To Have and Have Not*. Woolf: *The Years*.

CHRONOLOGY

Argentina: Irigoyen is removed in conservative coup led by General José F. Uriburi, who installs a repressive regime. Rebellion in Peru and revolt in Brazil. France begins Maginot Line. Gandhi undertakes civil disobedience campaign in India. Construction of Empire State Building in US.

El Salvador: General Hernández crushes the Salvadorean peasant movement and becomes dictator to 1944 till popular disgust at his brutality forces him to resign. Honduras: General Tiburcio Carías Andino establishes stranglehold on Honduran politics, crushing numerous peasant revolts. His domination of Honduras lasts until 1948. Peru: Emergency rule introduced. Argentina: Radical Party barred from elections. Britain abandons Gold Standard. Invention of the electric razor. Revolution in Spain.

US navy on stand-by during the *matanza* in El Salvador. Chile: Radical military coup removes ineffectual Liberal President. Brazil: 'Constitutionalist Revolution'. Armed conflict between Colombia and Peru. The Chaco War between Bolivia and Paraguay (to 1935) – 250,000 casualties. Nazis become largest single party in German Reichstag.

US: President Franklin Roosevelt initiates the 'good neighbour' policy and announces 'New Deal'. Nicaragua: Guerrilla resistance against conservative forces and US Marines. Hitler appointed Chancellor of Germany.

Mexico: Formation of the Mexican Labour Confederation, stimulating the expropriation of land for redistribution and the nationalization of oil assets. Brazil: Failed communist rebellion.

Chile: General strike, suspension of Congress, introduction of martial law. Spanish Civil War (to 1939). Death of George V in UK followed by abdication crisis of Edward VIII.

Argentina: Roberto Ortíz elected President. Brazil: Suspension of payments on all foreign debts, abolition of all existing political parties. Chamberlain Prime Minister in UK. First jet engine constructed. Japanese invade China. Amelia Earhart lost on Pacific flight. Zeppelin, *Hindenburg*, destroyed by fire when landing at Lakehurst, US.

DATE	AUTHOR'S LIFE	LITERARY CONTEXT
1938	Death of Jorge Borges, B's father. Suffers an accident and contracts septicemia. Writes his first Borgesian story, 'Pierre Menard, Author of *Don Quixote*', to see whether his brain has fully recovered after his illness.	Beckett: *Murphy*. Sartre: *Nausea*. Cummings: *Collected Poems*. Greene: *Brighton Rock*. Suicide of Leopoldo Lugones, Argentina's leading poet.
1939		Joyce: *Finnegans Wake*.
1940		Bioy Casares: *The Invention of Morel*. Greene: *The Power and the Glory*. Hemingway: *For Whom the Bell Tolls*.
1941	*The Garden of Forking Paths* published, containing the first eight stories of *Ficciones*.	
1942	Publication of a collection of spoof detective stories, *Seis problemas para Don Isidro Parodi* (Six Problems for Don Isidro Parodi), B's first collaboration with Adolfo Bioy Casares, a younger Argentinian writer of tastes very close to his own.	Camus: *The Stranger*. Eliot: *The Four Quartets*. Reyes: *La Experiencia literaria*.
1943		Sartre: *Being and Nothingness*.
1944	*Artifices*, a second collection of stories which, added to *The Garden of Forking Paths*, creates the first edition of *Ficciones*, later to be enlarged.	Camus: *Caligula*. Sartre: *Huis Clos*.
1945		Sartre: *The Roads to Freedom* (to 1947).
1946	'Promoted' by the Perón regime to 'the inspectorship of poultry and rabbits in the public markets'. Starts teaching English literature at the Asociación Argentina de Cultura Inglesa and lecturing on American literature in a Buenos Aires college.	Auerbach: *Mimesis*.

CHRONOLOGY

HISTORICAL EVENTS

Nazi activity in Chile. Italian Manifesto defines principles of Fascist Radicalism; first anti-Jewish measures in Italy. Resignation of Eden over Chamberlain's policy towards Mussolini. Hitler assumes command of German army. Spanish Republican victory at River Ebro.

Peru has its first civilian President for ten years – Manuel Prado. Paraguay negotiates reconstruction loan from US. German invasion of Czechoslovakia; World War II.
Resignation of Chamberlain in UK; Churchill Prime Minister. Paris occupied by Germans. Government of unoccupied France moved to Vichy. Assassination of Trotsky in Mexico.

Japanese attack Pearl Harbor.

Argentina: Ramón S. Castillo succeeds Roberto Ortíz as President. Rommel defeated by Montgomery at El Alamein. Hitler declares himself Germany's supreme 'Law Lord'.

Argentina: President Castillo is removed in military coup led by Brigadier General Arturo Rawson. Military rule in Argentina until 1946.
Political unrest in El Salvador. Attempted military coup in Colombia.
Allied landings in Normandy; German retreat; liberation of Paris.
Roosevelt elected for fourth term in US.

Brazil: Bloodless coup removes Getulio Vargas, President since 1930.
Unconditional surrender of Germany. Suicide of Hitler. Atomic bomb dropped on Hiroshima. Foundation of United Nations. Truman President of US; Attlee Prime Minister of UK.
Juan Domingo Perón President of Argentina (to 1955).

FICCIONES

DATE	AUTHOR'S LIFE	LITERARY CONTEXT
1947		Lorca: *Three Tragedies.* Gramsci: *Letters from Prison.* Quasimodo: *Day After Day.* Camus: *The Plague.* Mann: *Doktor Faustus.* Nabokov: *Bend Sinister.*
1948		Sartre: *What is Literature?.* Asturias: *El Señor Presidente.*
1949	*The Aleph*, B's second major collection of stories.	Paz: *Freedom on Parole.* Carpentier: *The Kingdom of this World.* de Beauvoir: *The Second Sex.* Orwell: *Nineteen Eighty-Four.*
1950	Elected President of the anti-Peronist Argentinian Society of Authors.	
1951		Beckett: *Molloy* and *Malone Dies.* Cortázar: *Bestiario.*
1952	*Otras inquisiciones* (Other Inquisitions), the principal collection of his essays.	Beckett: *Waiting for Godot.*
1953		Carpentier: *The Lost Steps.* Barthes: *Writing Degree Zero.* Robbe-Grillet: *The Erasers.* Beckett: *Watt.* Heidegger: *Being and Time.* Wittgenstein: *Philosophical Investigations.*
1954		
1955	The fall of Perón makes it possible for B. to be appointed Director of the National Library in Buenos Aires.	Lampedusa: *The Leopard.* Gómez de la Serna: *Total de greguerías.*
1956	Becomes Professor of English and American Literature at the University of Buenos Aires.	Camus: *The Fall.*

CHRONOLOGY

Argentina: Women gain vote. Formation of General Agreement on Tariffs and Trade (GATT). US aid for European postwar recovery. First report of flying saucers in US. Pilotless US plane crosses Atlantic. Christian Dior's 'New Look'.

Argentina: The Peronist Party wins a majority in Congressional Elections. Assassination of Gandhi. South Africa adopts *apartheid* as official policy. Russian blockade of West Berlin; Allied 'Air Lift'; Communist coup in Czechoslovakia; foundation of Israel.

Argentina: Temporary Constitution (to 1957) drafted replacing 1853 Constitution allowing Perón a second term in office and increasing the control of central government over the national economy. Foundation of NATO. Russian blockade of Berlin lifted; Communist regime established in Hungary.

Peru: General Odría assumes Presidency in uncontested election. Brazil: Vargas elected President, ruling until his suicide in 1954. India declares herself independent Republic within the British Commonwealth. Beginning of McCarthy era. Korean War (to 1953).

Argentina: Perón re-elected and maintains majority in Congress. Guy Burgess and Donald Maclean defect to Russia. Churchill re-elected in UK. Coup d'état in Cuba, General Batista returns to power. Bolivia: social revolution led by the tin miners' union and labour confederation ousts the government. Death in UK of King George VI; accession of Elizabeth II. Eisenhower US President. First contraceptive pill made. Construction begins of first atomic-powered submarine.

Colombia: Conservative Party removed in bloodless coup. Tito becomes President of Yugoslavia. Discovery of DNA.

Argentina: Peronism continues to dominate Argentinian politics in general elections. Guatemala: CIA-sponsored invasion removes pro-Communist President. Berlin Conference of Britain, France, US and Russia; Russia rejects proposals to reunify Germany. Communist Party outlawed in US.

Argentina: Leading sectors of army and navy combine with some air-force units to oust Perón. Five-man junta assumes dictatorial power. Bitter rivalry between the military elite. Eduardo Leonardi President of Argentina from September to November. Pedro Eugenio Arumburu President of Argentina (to 1958). Resignation of Churchill; Eden Prime Minister. Britain and US sign Atomic Energy agreement.

Chile: Left-wing parties form an electoral alliance. Eisenhower President of US. Suez Crisis.

FICCIONES

DATE	AUTHOR'S LIFE	LITERARY CONTEXT
1957		Paz: *Sun Stone*. Nabokov: *Pnin*. Barthes: *Mythologies*. Beckett: *Endgame*.
1958		Carpentier: *The War of Time*. Nabokov: *Lolita*. Pasternak: *Doctor Zhivago*. Beckett: *The Unnameable*.
1959		Burroughs: *The Naked Lunch*.
1960	Publishes *El Hacedor* (The Maker), a collection of short prose pieces and poems, 'my most personal work and, to my taste, maybe my best'.	Guevara: *Guerrilla Warfare*.
1961	Half-share (with Samuel Beckett) in the Formentor Prize launches B. on the way to international celebrity. Invited as Visiting Professor to the University of Texas.	García Márquez: *No-one Writes to the Colonel*. Sábato: *Sobre heroes y tumbas*. Onetti: *El astillero*.
1962		Fuentes: *The Death of Artemio Cruz*. Nabokov: *Pale Fire*. Beckett: *Happy Days*. Vargas Llosa: *La Ciudad y los perros*. Carpentier: *Explosion in a Cathedral*.
1963	Visit to Britain under the auspices of the British Council.	Guevara: *Reminiscences of the Cuban Revolutionary War*. Cortázar: *Hopscotch*. Primo Levi: *The Truce*.
1964	*El Otro, el mismo*, a collection of poems.	Sartre: *Words*.
1965		Onetti: *Juntacadáveres*. Calvino: *Cosmicomics*.
1966		Barthes: *Criticism and Truth*.
1967	Gives the Charles Eliot Norton lectures at Harvard University. Marries Elsa Astete Millán, a widow whom he had known as a young girl.	Derrida: *Of Grammatology*. Primo Levi: *Natural Stories*. García Márquez: *One Hundred Years of Solitude*. Cabrera Infante: *Three Trapped Tigers*.

CHRONOLOGY

Treaty of Rome sets up European Economic Community: France, Italy, West Germany, Belgium, Holland and Luxembourg.

Arturo Frondizi President of Argentina (to 1962); return to civilian politics.

Cuba: Batista overthrown by Fidel Castro's guerrillas. New government formed in Havana.
Argentina: Peronist Party barred from participation in elections. Cuba: Re-establishment of diplomatic relations with USSR. Brezhnev becomes President of USSR. John F. Kennedy elected President of US.

'Papa Doc' consolidates his regime in Haiti. US severs relations with Cuba; 'Bay of Pigs'. Construction of Berlin Wall. Yuri Gagarin becomes first man in space.

Argentina: President Frondizi alienates the military hierarchy by permitting Peronist participation in Congressional elections. Peronists win a majority but Frondizi is pressurized by the military to nullify election results in provinces where Peronism is successful. The military removes Frondizi and installs the Leader of the Senate, José Maria Guido, who becomes acting President of Argentina (to 1963). Peru: Military junta seizes power. Cuba: USSR supplies arms to Castro's government. Cuban Missile Crisis.
Arturo Umberto Illia President of Argentina (to 1966); introduction of proportional representation. Assassination of John F. Kennedy.

Brazil: Military coup ushering in long period of dictatorship. Chile: Left-wing coalition defeated by Christian Democrats. Cuba: Castro visits Moscow.
US begins bombing of North Vietnam.

Hard-line junta led by Juan Carlos Onganía seizes power in Argentina (to 1970). Mao launches 'Cultural Revolution' in China.
Military coup in Peru; suspension of Congress in Brazil. France blocks Britain's entry into Common Market. Six Day War between Israel and Arab states. First successful heart transplant.

DATE	AUTHOR'S LIFE	LITERARY CONTEXT
1968		Solzhenitsyn: *Cancer Ward.*
1969	*Elogio de la sombra* (In Praise of Darkness), more poems, his fifth collection.	Puig: *Heartbreak Tango.* Vargas Llosa: *Conversation in the Cathedral.*
1970	*El Informe de Brodie* (Brodie's Report), his third collection of stories. Divorces Elsa and returns to live with his mother.	Barthes: *S/Z.* Foucault: *The Order of Things.*
1971	Receives an honorary degree from the University of Oxford.	Primo Levi: *A Structural Defect.*
1972		
1973	Resigns from the directorship of the National Library.	Dorfman: *Hard Rain.* Puig: *The Buenos Aires Affair.* Barthes: *The Pleasure of the Text.* Derrida: *Margins of Philosophy.*
1974		Carpentier: *Reasons of State.*
1975	*El Libro de arena* (The Book of Sand), a fourth and final collection of stories. Mother dies, aged ninety-nine.	Paz: *The Monkey Grammarian.* Fuentes: *Terra Nostra.* Primo Levi: *The Periodic Table.* Foucault: *Discipline and Punish.*
1976		Barthes: *A Lover's Discourse.*
1977		Primo Levi: *The Wrench.*
1979		Calvino: *If on a winter's night a traveller.*
1980		
1981		Vargas Llosa: *The War of the End of the World.* Timerman: *Prisoner Without a Name, Cell Without a Number.*
1982		Allende: *The House of the Spirits.* Primo Levi: *If Not Now, When?* García Márquez: *Chronicle of a Death Foretold.*

CHRONOLOGY

Treaty on non-proliferation of nuclear weapons signed by 61 countries (Cuba refuses to sign). Russian invasion of Czechoslovakia. Paris: Students in anti-government riots. Assassination of Martin Luther King. Nixon President in US.

Argentina: Military suppression of the *Cordobazo* – a mass insurrection in the city of Córdoba – prompts resignation of five ministers. Resignation of de Gaulle in France; succeeded by Pompidou. Americans land man on moon.

Argentina: Military junta in office between June 8–18. Roberto Marcelo Levingstón President of Argentina (to 1971); terrorist murder of former President Pedro Aramburu. USSR accuses Nixon administration of developing 'war psychosis'. US forces attack Communist bases in Cambodia. Edward Heath Prime Minister in UK.

Argentina: Military junta in office from March 22–5. Alejandro Agustín Lanusse President of Argentina (to 1973).

El Salvador: Military oppose free elections. Strategic Arms Limitation Treaty (SALT) signed by US and USSR.

Hector José Campora President of Argentina from May to July; Raúl Lastiri acting President from July to October; Perón returns as President (to 1974). Cuba and US sign a five-year anti-hijacking pact to apply to aircraft and vessels. Cuba and Argentina renew diplomatic relations.

Maria Estela Martínez de Perón President of Argentina (to 1976). Brezhnev visits Cuba. Nixon resigns as US President.

Cuba and West Germany renew diplomatic relations. End of Vietnam War.

Argentina: Chaotic Peronist government is removed by a military coup. A series of military dictatorships rule Argentina until 1983 – mass arrests, torture and political murder; 15,000 people disappear during military rule. Jorge Rafael Videla President of Argentina (to 1981). Cuba: Castro declares hijacking agreement void from 1977. Death of Mao Tse Tung.

US government lifts ban on travel to Cuba. Cuba and Spain sign scientific and technical agreement.

Pressures for democratic elections in Brazil. Margaret Thatcher becomes first woman Prime Minister in UK.

Formation of Solidarity Union in Poland.

Roberto Viola President of Argentina from March to December; Leopoldo Galtieri President (to 1982). Ronald Reagan elected President in US.

Argentina: Invasion of the Falkland Islands. Britain declares a naval exclusion zone around the islands. British navy sinks the Argentinian cruiser *Belgrano* on orders from the War Cabinet. General Galtieri rejects Peruvian peace plan. British force despatched from Ascension Island retakes islands. Borges' description of the war: 'Two bald men fighting over a comb.' Reynaldo Bignone President of Argentina (to 1983).

DATE	AUTHOR'S LIFE	LITERARY CONTEXT
1983	Decorated with the Légion d'Honneur.	Dorfman: *The Last Song of Manuel Sendero*.
1984		Allende: *Of Love and Shadows*.
1985		Primo Levi: *The Drowned and the Saved*.
1986	Married for a second time, to María Kodama. Dies on June 14 in Geneva, aged eighty-six.	

CHRONOLOGY

Argentina: Raúl Alfonsín Foulkes is elected President in return to civilian rule. He enjoys a 'honeymoon' period but is unable to cope with pressures due to deep-rooted economic problems and the aftermath of the 'Malvinas' (Falklands) disaster. US invasion of Grenada. Reagan calls USSR an 'evil empire' and proposes 'Star Wars'.

CIA initiates mining of Nicaraguan ports. The Sandinista government takes its case to the World Court. Economic aid guaranteed by US to El Salvador. Pinochet re-introduces state of siege in Chile. Famine in Ethiopia.

US initiates a three-year trade embargo against the Sandinista government.

Argentina: President Alfonsín rushes a 'final point' Bill through Congress designed to prevent further prosecution of military personnel. Peru: Military massacre of three hundred prisoners during prison unrest.

CONTENTS

PART ONE

THE GARDEN
OF FORKING PATHS

(1941)

PROLOGUE

The eight pieces of this book do not require extraneous elucidation. The eighth piece, 'The Garden of Forking Paths', is a detective story; its readers will assist at the execution, and all the preliminaries, of a crime, a crime whose purpose will not be unknown to them, but which they will not understand – it seems to me – until the last paragraph. The other pieces are fantasies. One of them, 'The Babylon Lottery', is not entirely innocent of symbolism.

I am not the first author of the narrative titled 'The Library of Babel'; those curious to know its history and its prehistory may interrogate a certain page of Number 59 of the journal *Sur*,* which records the heterogeneous names of Leucippus and Lasswitz, of Lewis Carroll and Aristotle. In 'The Circular Ruins' everything is unreal. In 'Pierre Menard, Author of Don Quixote', what is unreal is the destiny imposed upon himself by the protagonist. The list of writings I attribute to him is not too amusing but neither is it arbitrary; it constitutes a diagram of his mental history. . . .

The composition of vast books is a laborious and impoverishing extravagance. To go on for five hundred pages developing an idea whose perfect oral exposition is possible in a few minutes! A better course of procedure is to pretend that these books already exist, and then to offer a résumé, a commentary. Thus proceeded Carlyle in *Sartor Resartus*. Thus Butler in *The Fair Haven*. These are works which suffer the imperfection of being themselves books, and of being no less tautological than the others. More reasonable, more inept, more indolent, I have preferred to write notes upon imaginary books. Such as 'Tlön, Uqbar, Orbis Tertius', 'An Examin-

* The great South American literary journal edited in Buenos Aires by Victoria Ocampo. – *Editor's note.*

ation of the Work of Herbert Quain', 'The Approach to Al-Mu'tasim'. The last-named dates from 1935. Recently I read *The Sacred Fount* (1901), whose general argument is perhaps analogous. The narrator, in James's delicate novel, investigates whether or not B is influenced by A or C; in 'The Approach to Al-Mu'tasim' the narrator feels a presentiment or divines through B the extremely remote existence of Z, whom B does not know.

Buenos Aires
10 November, 1941   J.L.B.

TLÖN, UQBAR, ORBIS TERTIUS

I owe the discovery of Uqbar to the conjunction of a mirror and an encyclopedia. The unnerving mirror hung at the end of a corridor in a villa on Calle Goana, in Ramos Mejía; the misleading encyclopedia goes by the name of *The Anglo-American Cyclopaedia* (New York, 1917), and is a literal if inadequate reprint of the 1902 *Encyclopaedia Britannica*. The whole affair happened some five years ago. Bioy Casares had dined with me that night and talked to us at length about a great scheme for writing a novel in the first person, using a narrator who omitted or corrupted what happened and who ran into various contradictions, so that only a handful of readers, a very small handful, would be able to decipher the horrible or banal reality behind the novel. From the far end of the corridor, the mirror was watching us; and we discovered, with the inevitability of discoveries made late at night, that mirrors have something grotesque about them. Then Bioy Casares recalled that one of the heresiarchs of Uqbar had stated that mirrors and copulation are abominable, since they both multiply the numbers of man. I asked him the source of that memorable sentence, and he replied that it was recorded in the *Anglo-American Cyclopaedia*, in its article on Uqbar. It so happened that the villa (which we had rented furnished) possessed a copy of that work. In the final pages of Volume XLVI, we ran across an article on Upsala; in the beginning of Volume XLVII, we found one on Ural-Altaic languages; but not one word on Uqbar. A little put out, Bioy consulted the index volumes. In vain he tried every possible spelling – Ukbar, Ucbar, Ooqbar, Ookbar, Oukbahr. ... Before leaving, he informed me it was a region in either Iraq or Asia Minor. I must say that I acknowledged this a little uneasily. I supposed that this undocumented country and its anonymous heresiarch had been deliberately invented by Bioy out of modesty, to substantiate a phrase. A futile examination of one of the atlases of Justus Perthes strengthened my doubt.

On the following day, Bioy telephoned me from Buenos Aires. He told me that he had in front of him the article on Uqbar, in Volume XLVI of the encyclopedia. It did not specify the name of the heresiarch, but it did note his doctrine, in words almost identical to the ones he had repeated to me, though, I would say, inferior from a literary point of view. He had remembered: 'Copulation and mirrors are abominable.' The text of the encyclopedia read: 'For one of those gnostics, the visible universe was an illusion or, more precisely, a sophism. Mirrors and fatherhood are abominable because they multiply it and extend it.' I said, in all sincerity, that I would like to see that article. A few days later, he brought it. This surprised me, because the scrupulous cartographic index of Ritter's *Erdkunde* completely failed to mention the name of Uqbar.

The volume which Bioy brought was indeed Volume XLVI of *The Anglo-American Cyclopaedia*. On the title page and spine, the alphabetical key was the same as in our copy, but instead of 917 pages, it had 921. These four additional pages consisted of the article on Uqbar – not accounted for by the alphabetical cipher, as the reader will have noticed. We ascertained afterwards that there was no other difference between the two volumes. Both, as I think I pointed out, are reprints of the tenth *Encyclopaedia Britannica*. Bioy had acquired his copy in one of a number of book sales.

We read the article with some care. The passage remembered by Bioy was perhaps the only startling one. The rest seemed probable enough, very much in keeping with the general tone of the work and, naturally, a little dull. Reading it over, we discovered, beneath the superficial authority of the prose, a fundamental vagueness. Of the fourteen names mentioned in the geographical section, we recognized only three – Khurasan, Armenia, and Erzurum – and they were dragged into the text in a strangely ambiguous way. Among the historical names, we recognized only one, that of the imposter, Smerdis the Magian, and it was invoked in a rather metaphorical sense. The notes appeared to fix precisely the frontiers of Uqbar, but the points of reference were all, vaguely enough, rivers and craters and mountain chains in that same region. We read, for instance, that the southern frontier is defined by the lowlands of Tsai Haldun and the Axa delta, and that wild horses flourish in the islands of that delta. This, at the top of page 918. In the historical section (page 920), we gathered that, just after the religious persecutions of the thirteenth century, the orthodox sought refuge in the islands, where their obelisks have survived, and where it is a common enough occurrence to dig up one of their stone mirrors. The language and literature section was brief. There was one notable characteristic: it remarked that the literature of Uqbar was fantastic in character, and that its epics and legends never referred to reality, but to the two imaginary regions of Mlejnas and Tlön. . . . The bibliography listed four volumes, which we have not yet come across, even although the third – Silas Haslam: *History of the Land Called Uqbar*, 1874 – appears in the library catalogues of Bernard Quaritch.* The first, *Lesbare und lesenswerthe Bemerkungen über das Land Ukkbar in Klein-Asien*, is dated 1641, and is a work of Johann Valentin Andreä. The fact is significant; a couple of years later I ran across that name accidentally in the thirteenth volume of De Quincey's *Writings*, and I knew that it was the name of a German theologian who, at the beginning of the seventeenth century, described the imaginary community of Rosae Crucis – the community which was later founded by others in imitation of the one he had preconceived.

That night, we visited the National Library. Fruitlessly we exhausted atlases, catalogues, yearbooks of geographical societies, memoirs of travellers and historians – nobody had ever been in Uqbar. Neither did the general index of Bioy's encyclopedia show the name. The following day, Carlos Mastronardi, to whom I had referred the whole business,

---

* Haslam has also published *A General History of Labyrinths*.

caught sight, in a Corrientes and Talcahuano bookshop, of the black and gold bindings of *The Anglo-American Cyclopaedia*. ... He went in and looked up Volume XLVI. Naturally, there was not the slightest mention of Uqbar.

II

Some small fading memory of one Herbert Ashe, an engineer for the southern railroads, hangs on in the hotel in Androgué, between the luscious honeysuckle and the illusory depths of the mirrors. In life, he suffered from a sense of unreality, as do so many Englishmen; dead, he is not even the ghostly creature he was then. He was tall and languid; his limp squared beard had once been red. He was, I understand, a widower, and childless. Every so many years, he went to England to visit – judging by the photographs he showed us – a sundial and some oak trees. My father and he had cemented (the verb is excessive) one of those English friendships which begin by avoiding intimacies and eventually eliminate speech altogether. They used to exchange books and periodicals; they would beat one another at chess, without saying a word. ... I remember him in the corridor of the hotel, a mathematics textbook in his hand, gazing now and again at the passing colours of the sky. One afternoon, we discussed the duodecimal numerical system (in which twelve is written 10). Ashe said that as a matter of fact, he was transcribing some duodecimal tables, I forget which, into sexagesimals (in which sixty is written 10), adding that this work had been commissioned by a Norwegian in Rio Grande do Sul. We had known him for eight years and he had never mentioned having stayed in that part of the country. ... We spoke of rural life, of *capangas*, of the Brazilian etymology of the word *gaucho* (which some old people in the east still pronounce *gaúcho*), and nothing more was said – God forgive me – of duodecimal functions. In September, 1937 (we ourselves were not at the hotel at the time), Herbert Ashe died of an aneurysmal rupture. Some days before, he had received from Brazil a stamped, registered package. It was a book, an octavo volume.

Ashe left it in the bar where, months later, I found it. I began to leaf through it and felt a sudden curious lightheadedness, which I will not go into, since this is the story, not of my particular emotions, but of Uqbar and Tlön and Orbis Tertius. In the Islamic world, there is one night, called the Night of Nights, on which the secret gates of the sky open wide and the water in the water jugs tastes sweeter; if those gates were to open, I would not feel what I felt that afternoon. The book was written in English, and had 1001 pages. On the yellow leather spine, and again on the title page, I read these words: *A First Encyclopaedia of Tlön*. Volume XI. Hlaer to Jangr. There was nothing to indicate either date or place of origin. On the first page and on a sheet of silk paper covering one of the coloured engravings there was a blue oval stamp with the inscription: ORBIS TERTIUS. It was two years since I had discovered, in a volume of a pirated encyclopedia, a brief description of a false country; now, chance was showing me something much more valuable, something to be reckoned with. Now, I had in my hands a substantial fragment of the complete history of an unknown planet, with its architecture and its playing cards, its mythological terrors and the sound of its dialects, its emperors and its oceans, its minerals, its birds, and its fishes, its algebra and its fire, its theological and metaphysical arguments, all clearly stated, coherent, without any apparent dogmatic intention or parodic undertone.

The eleventh volume of which I speak refers to both subsequent and preceding volumes. Néstor Ibarra, in an article (in the *N.R.F.*) now a classic, has denied the existence of those corollary volumes; Ezequiel Martínez Estrada and Drieu La Rochelle have, I think, succeeded in refuting this doubt. The fact is that, up until now, the most patient investigations have proved fruitless. We have turned the libraries of Europe, North and South America upside down – in vain. Alfonso Reyes, bored with the tedium of this minor detective work, proposes that we all take on the task of reconstructing the missing volumes, many and vast as they were: *ex ungue leonem*. He calculates, half seriously, that one generation of Tlönists would be enough. This bold estimate brings us back to the basic problem: who were the people who had invented Tlön? The plural is unavoidable, because we have unanimously rejected the idea of a single creator, some transcendental Leibnitz working in modest obscurity. We conjecture that this 'brave new world' was the work of a secret society of astronomers, biologists, engineers, metaphysicians, poets, chemists, mathematicians, moralists, painters, and geometricians, all under the supervision of an unknown genius. There are plenty of individuals who have mastered these various disciplines without having any facility for invention, far less for submitting that inventiveness to a strict, systematic plan. This plan is so vast that each individual contribution to it is infinitesimal. To begin with, Tlön was thought to be nothing more than a chaos, a free and irresponsible work of the imagination; now it was clear that it is a complete cosmos, and that the strict laws which govern it have been carefully formulated, albeit provisionally. It is enough to note that the apparent contradictions in the eleventh volume are the basis for proving the existence of the others, so lucid and clear is the scheme maintained in it. The popular magazines have publicized, with pardonable zeal, the zoology and topography of Tlön. I think, however, that its transparent tigers and its towers of blood scarcely deserve the unwavering attention of *all* men. I should like to take some little time to deal with its conception of the universe.

Hume remarked once and for all that the arguments of Berkeley were not only thoroughly unanswerable but thoroughly unconvincing. This dictum is emphatically true as it applies to our world; but it falls down completely in Tlön. The nations of that planet are congenitally idealist. Their language, with its derivatives – religion, literature, and metaphysics – presupposes idealism. For them, the world is not a concurrence of objects in space, but a heterogeneous series of independent acts. It is serial and temporal, but not spatial. There are no nouns in the hypothetical *Ursprache* of Tlön, which is the source of the living language and the dialects; there are impersonal verbs qualified by monosyllabic suffixes or prefixes which have the force of adverbs. For example, there is no word corresponding to the noun *moon*, but there is a verb *to moon* or *to moondle*. *The moon rose over the sea* would be written *hlör u fang axaxaxas mlö*, or, to put it in order: *upward beyond the constant flow there was moondling*. (Xul Solar translates it succinctly: *upward, behind the onstreaming it mooned*.)

The previous passage refers to the languages of the southern hemisphere. In those of the northern hemisphere (the eleventh volume has little information on its *Ursprache*), the basic unit is not the verb, but the monosyllabic adjective. Nouns are formed by an accumulation of adjectives. One does not say moon; one says *airy-clear over dark-round* or *orange-faint-of-sky* or some other accumulation. In the chosen example, the mass of adjectives corresponds to a real object. The happening is completely fortuitous. In the literature of this hemisphere (as in the lesser world of Meinong), ideal objects abound, invoked and dissolved momentarily, according to poetic necessity. Sometimes, the faintest simultaneousness brings them about. There are objects made up of two sense elements, one visual, the other auditory – the colour of a sunrise and the distant call of a bird. Other objects are made up of many elements – the sun, the water against the swimmer's chest, the vague quivering pink which one sees when the eyes are closed, the feeling of being swept away by a river or by sleep. These second degree objects can be combined with others; using certain abbreviations, the process is practically an infinite one. There are famous poems made up of one enormous word, a word which in truth forms a poetic *object*, the creation of the writer. The fact that no one believes that nouns refer to an actual reality means, paradoxically enough, that there is no limit to the numbers of them. The languages of the northern hemisphere of Tlön include all the names in Indo-European languages – plus a great many others.

It is no exaggeration to state that in the classical culture of Tlön, there is only one discipline, that of psychology. All others are subordinated to it. I have remarked that the men of that planet conceive of the universe as a series of mental processes, whose unfolding is to be understood only as a time sequence. Spinoza attributes to the inexhaustibly divine in man the qualities of extension and of thinking. In Tlön, nobody would understand the juxtaposition of the first, which is only characteristic of certain states of being, with the second, which is a perfect synonym for the cosmos. To put it another way – they do not conceive of the spatial as everlasting in time. The perception of a cloud of smoke on the horizon and, later, of the countryside on fire and, later, of a half-extinguished cigar which caused the conflagration would be considered an example of the association of ideas.

This monism, or extreme idealism, completely invalidates science. To explain or to judge an event is to identify or unite it with another one. In Tlön, such connexion is a later stage in the mind of the observer, which can in no way affect or illuminate the earlier stage. Each state of mind is irreducible. The mere act of giving it a name, that is of classifying it, implies a falsification of it. From all this, it would be possible to deduce that there is no science in Tlön, let alone rational thought. The paradox, however, is that sciences exist, in countless number. In philosophy, the same thing happens as happens with the nouns in the northern hemisphere. The fact that any philosophical system is bound in advance to be a dialectical game, a *Philosophie des Als Ob*, means that systems abound, unbelievable systems, beautifully constructed or else sensational in effect. The metaphysicians of Tlön are not looking for truth, nor even for an approximation of it; they are after a kind of amazement. They consider metaphysics a branch of fantastic literature. They know that a system is nothing more than the subordination of all the aspects of the universe to some one of them. Even the phrase 'all the aspects' can be rejected, since it presupposes the impossible inclusion of the present moment, and of past moments. Even so, the plural 'past moments' is inadmissible, since it supposes another impossible operation. ... One of the schools in Tlön has reached the point of denying time. It reasons that the present is undefined, that the future has no other reality than as present hope, that the past is no more than present memory.* Another school declares that the *whole of time* has already happened and that our life is a vague memory or dim reflection, doubtless false and fragmented, of an irrevocable process. Another school has it that the history of the universe, which contains the history of our lives and the most tenuous details of them, is the handwriting produced by a minor god in order to communicate with a demon. Another maintains that the universe is comparable to those code systems in which not all the symbols have meaning, and in which only that which happens every three hundredth night is true. Another believes that, while we are asleep here, we are awake somewhere else, and that thus every man is two men.

Among the doctrines of Tlön, none has occasioned greater scandal than the doctrine of materialism. Some thinkers have formulated it with less clarity than zeal, as one might put forward a paradox. To clarify the general understanding of this unlikely thesis, one eleventh century† heresiarch offered the parable of nine copper coins, which enjoyed in Tlön the same noisy reputation as did the Eleatic paradoxes of Zeno in their day. There are many versions of this 'feat of specious reasoning' which vary the number of coins and the number of discoveries. Here is the commonest:

On Tuesday, X ventures along a deserted road and loses nine copper coins. On Thursday, Y finds on the road four coins, somewhat rusted by Wednesday's rain. On Friday, Z comes across three coins on the road. On Friday morning, X finds two coins in the corridor of his house. [The heresiarch is trying to deduce from this story the reality, that is, the continuity, of the nine recovered coins.] It is absurd, he states, to suppose that four of the coins have not existed between Tuesday and Thursday, three between Tuesday and

* Russell (*The Analysis of Mind*, 1921, page 159) conjectures that our planet was created a few moments ago, and provided with a humanity which 'remembers' an illusory past.
† A century, in accordance with the duodecimal system, signifies a period of one hundred and forty-four years.

Friday afternoon, and two between Tuesday and Friday morning. It is logical to assume that they *have* existed, albeit in some secret way, in a manner whose understanding is concealed from men, in every moment, in all three places.

The language of Tlön is by its nature resistant to the formulation of this paradox; most people do not understand it. At first, the defenders of common sense confined themselves to denying the truth of the anecdote. They declared that it was a verbal fallacy, based on the reckless use of two neological expressions, not substantiated by common usage, and contrary to the laws of strict thought – the verbs *to find* and *to lose* entail a *petitio principii*, since they presuppose that the first nine coins and the second are identical. They recalled that any noun – *man, money, Thursday, Wednesday, rain* – has only metaphorical value. They denied the misleading detail 'somewhat rusted by Wednesday's rain', since it assumes what must be demonstrated – the continuing existence of the four coins between Thursday and Tuesday. They explained that equality is one thing and identity another, and formulated a kind of *reductio ad absurdum*, the hypothetical case of nine men who, on nine successive nights, suffer a violent pain. Would it not be ridiculous, they asked, to claim that this pain is the same one each time?* They said that the heresiarch was motivated mainly by the blasphemous intention of attributing the divine category of *being* to some ordinary coins; and that sometimes he was denying plurality, at other times not. They argued thus: that if equality entails identity, it would have to be admitted at the same time that the nine coins are only one coin.

Amazingly enough, these refutations were not conclusive. After the problem had been stated and restated for a hundred years, one thinker no less brilliant than the heresiarch himself, but in the orthodox tradition, advanced a most daring

---

* Nowadays, one of the churches of Tlön maintains platonically that such and such a pain, such and such a greenish-yellow colour, such and such a temperature, such and such a sound, etc., make up the only reality there is. All men, in the climactic instant of coitus, are the same man. All men who repeat one line of Shakespeare *are* William Shakespeare.

hypothesis. This felicitous supposition declared that there is only one Individual, and that this indivisible Individual is every one of the separate beings in the universe, and that those beings are the instruments and masks of divinity itself. X is Y and is Z. Z finds three coins because he remembers that X lost them. X finds only two in the corridor because he remembers that the others have been recovered. ... The eleventh volume gives us to understand that there were three principal reasons which led to the complete victory of this pantheistic idealism. First, it repudiated solipsism. Second, it made possible the retention of a psychological basis for the sciences. Third, it permitted the cult of the gods to be retained. Schopenhauer, the passionate and clear-headed Schopenhauer, advanced a very similar theory in the first volume of his *Parerga und Paralipomena*.

The geometry of Tlön has two somewhat distinct systems, a visual one and a tactile one. The latter system corresponds to our geometry; they consider it inferior to the former. The foundation of visual geometry is the surface, not the point. This system rejects the principle of parallelism, and states that, as man moves about, he alters the forms which surround him. The arithmetical system is based on the idea of indefinite numbers. It emphasizes the importance of the concepts *greater* and *lesser*, which our mathematicians symbolize as $\geqslant$ and $\leqslant$. It states that the operation of counting modifies quantities and changes them from indefinites into definites. The fact that several individuals counting the same quantity arrive at the same result is, say their psychologists, an example of the association of ideas or the good use of memory. We already know that in Tlön the source of all-knowing is single and eternal.

In literary matters too, the dominant notion is that everything is the work of one single author. Books are rarely signed. The concept of plagiarism does not exist; it has been established that all books are the work of one single writer, who is timeless and anonymous. Criticism is prone to invent authors. A critic will choose two dissimilar works – the *Tao Tê Ching* and *The Thousand and One Nights*, let us say – and attribute them to the same writer, and then with all probity explore the psychology of this interesting *homme de lettres*. . . . The books themselves are also odd. Works of fiction are based on a single plot, which runs through every imaginable permutation. Works of natural philosophy invariably include thesis and antithesis, the strict pro and con of a theory. A book which does not include its opposite, or 'counter-book', is considered incomplete.

Centuries and centuries of idealism have not failed to influence reality. In the very oldest regions of Tlön, it is not an uncommon occurrence for lost objects to be duplicated. Two people are looking for a pencil; the first one finds it and says nothing; the second finds a second pencil, no less real, but more in keeping with his expectation. These secondary objects are called *hrönir* and, even though awkward in form, are a little larger than the originals. Until recently, the *hrönir* were the accidental children of absent-mindedness and forgetfulness. It seems improbable that the methodical production of them has been going on for almost a hundred years, but so it is stated in the eleventh volume. The first attempts were fruitless. Nevertheless, the *modus operandi* is worthy of note. The director of one of the state prisons announced to the convicts that in an ancient river bed certain tombs were to be found, and promised freedom to any prisoner who made an important discovery. In the months preceding the excavation, printed photographs of what was to be found were shown the prisoners. The first attempt proved that hope and zeal could be inhibiting; a week of work with shovel and pick succeeded in unearthing no *hrön* other than a rusty wheel, postdating the experiment. This was kept a secret, and the experiment was later repeated in four colleges. In three of them the failure was almost complete; in the fourth (the director of which died by chance during the initial excavation), the students dug up – or produced – a gold mask, an archaic sword, two or three earthenware urns, and the moldered mutilated torso of a king with an inscription on his breast which has so far not been deciphered. Thus was discovered the unfitness of witnesses who were aware of the experimental nature of the search. . . .

Mass investigations produced objects which contradicted one another; now, individual projects, as far as possible spontaneous, are preferred. The methodical development of *hrönir*, states the eleventh volume, has been of enormous service to archaeologists. It has allowed them to question and even to modify the past, which nowadays is no less malleable or obedient than the future. One curious fact: the *hrönir* of the second and third degree – that is, the *hrönir* derived from another *hrön*, and the *hrönir* derived from the *hrön* of a *hrön* – exaggerate the flaws of the original; those of the fifth degree are almost uniform; those of the ninth can be confused with those of the second; and those of the eleventh degree have a purity of form which the originals do not possess. The process is a recurrent one; a *hrön* of the twelfth degree begins to deteriorate in quality. Stranger and more perfect than any *hrön* is sometimes the *ur*, which is a thing produced by suggestion, an object brought into being by hope. The great gold mask I mentioned previously is a distinguished example.

Things duplicate themselves in Tlön. They tend at the same time to efface themselves, to lose their detail when people forget them. The classic example is that of a stone threshold which lasted as long as it was visited by a beggar, and which faded from sight on his death. Occasionally, a few birds, a horse perhaps, have saved the ruins of an amphitheatre. (1940. *Salto Oriental.*)

Postscript. 1947. I reprint the foregoing article just as it appeared in the *Anthology of Fantastic Literature*, 1940, omitting no more than some figures of speech, and a kind of burlesque summing up, which now strikes me as frivolous. So many things have happened since that date. ... I will confine myself to putting them down.

In March, 1941, a manuscript letter by Gunnar Erfjord came to light in a volume of Hinton, which had belonged to Herbert Ashe. The envelope bore the postmark of Ouro Preto. The letter cleared up entirely the mystery of Tlön. The text of it confirmed Martínez Estrada's thesis. The elaborate story began one night in Lucerne or London, in the early seventeenth century. A benevolent secret society (which counted Dalgarno and, later, George Berkeley among its members) came together to invent a country. The first tentative plan gave prominence to 'hermetic studies', philanthropy, and the cabala. Andreä's curious book dates from that first period. At the end of some years of conventicles and premature syntheses, they realized that a single generation was not long enough in which to define a country. They made a resolution that each one of the master-scholars involved should elect a disciple to carry on the work. That hereditary arrangement prevailed; and after a hiatus of two centuries, the persecuted brotherhood reappeared in America. About 1824, in Memphis, Tennessee, one of the members had a conversation with the millionaire ascetic, Ezra Buckley. Buckley listened with some disdain as the other men talked, and then burst out laughing at the modesty of the project. He declared that in America it was absurd to invent a country, and proposed the invention of a whole planet. To this gigantic idea, he added another, born of his own nihilism* – that of keeping the enormous project a secret. The twenty volumes of the *Encyclopaedia Britannica* were then in circulation; Buckley suggested a systematic encyclopedia of the imaginary planet. He would leave the society his mountain ranges with their gold fields, his navigable rivers, his prairies where bull and bison roamed, his Negroes, his brothels, and his dollars, on one condition: 'The work will have no truck with the imposter Jesus Christ.' Buckley did not believe in God, but nevertheless wished to demonstrate to the nonexistent God that mortal men were capable of conceiving a world. Buckley was poisoned in Baton Rouge in 1828; in 1914, the society forwarded to its collaborators, three hundred in number, the final volume of the *First Encyclopaedia of Tlön*. The edition was secret; the forty volumes which comprised it (the work was vaster than any previously undertaken by men) were to be the basis for another work, more detailed, and this time written, not in English, but in some one of the languages of Tlön. This

---

* Buckley was a freethinker, a fatalist, and an apologist for slavery.

review of an illusory world was called, provisionally, *Orbis Tertius*, and one of its minor demiurges was Herbert Ashe, whether as an agent of Gunnar Erfjord, or as a full associate, I do not know. The fact that he received a copy of the eleventh volume would favour the second view. But what about the others? About 1942, events began to speed up. I recall with distinct clarity one of the first, and I seem to have felt something of its premonitory character. It occurred in an apartment on the Calle Laprida, facing a high open balcony which looked to the west. From Poitiers, the Princess of Faucigny Lucinge had received her silver table service. Out of the recesses of a crate, stamped all over with international markings, fine immobile pieces were emerging – silver plate from Utrecht and Paris, with hard heraldic fauna, a samovar. Amongst them, trembling faintly, just perceptibly, like a sleeping bird, was a magnetic compass. It shivered mysteriously. The princess did not recognize it. The blue needle longed for magnetic north. The metal case was concave. The letters on the dial corresponded to those of one of the alphabets of Tlön. Such was the first intrusion of the fantastic world into the real one. A disturbing accident brought it about that I was also witness to the second. It happened some months afterwards in a grocery store belonging to a Brazilian, in Cuchilla Negra. Amorim and I were on our way back from Sant'Anna. A sudden rising of the Tacuarembó river compelled us to test (and to suffer patiently) the rudimentary hospitality of the general store. The grocer set up some creaking cots for us in a large room, cluttered with barrels and wineskins. We went to bed, but were kept from sleeping until dawn by the drunkenness of an invisible neighbour, who alternated between shouting indecipherable abuse and singing snatches of *milongas*, or rather, snatches of the same *milonga*. As might be supposed, we attributed this insistent uproar to the fiery rum of the proprietor. ... At dawn, the man lay dead in the corridor. The coarseness of his voice had deceived us; he was a young boy. In his delirium, he had spilled a few coins and a shining metal cone, of the diameter of a die, from his heavy gaucho belt. A serving lad tried to pick up this cone – in vain. It was scarcely possible for a man to lift it. I held it in my hand for some minutes. I remember that it was intolerably heavy, and that after putting it down, its oppression remained. I also remember the precise circle it marked in my flesh. This manifestation of an object which was so tiny and at the same time so heavy left me with an unpleasant sense of abhorrence and fear. A countryman proposed that it be thrown into the rushing river. Amorim acquired it for a few pesos. No one knew anything of the dead man, only that 'he came from the frontier'. Those small and extremely heavy cones, made of a metal which does not exist in this world, are images of divinity in certain religions in Tlön.

Here I conclude the personal part of my narrative. The rest, when it is not in their hopes or their fears, is at least in the memories of all my readers. It is enough to recall or to mention subsequent events, in as few words as possible; that concave basin which is the collective memory will furnish the wherewithal to enrich or amplify them. About 1944, a reporter from the Nashville, Tennessee, *American* uncovered, in a Memphis library, the forty volumes of the *First Encyclopaedia of Tlön*. Even now it is uncertain whether this discovery was accidental, or whether the directors of the still nebulous *Orbis Tertius* condoned it. The second alternative is more likely. Some of the more improbable features of the eleventh volume (for example, the multiplying of the *hrönir*) had been either removed or modified in the Memphis copy. It is reasonable to suppose that these erasures were in keeping with the plan of projecting a world which would not be too incompatible with the real world. The dissemination of objects from Tlön throughout various countries would complement that plan. ...* The fact is that the international Press overwhelmingly hailed the 'find'. Manuals, anthologies, summaries, literal versions, authorized reprints, and pirated editions of the Master Work of Man poured and continue to pour out into the world. Almost immediately, reality gave

* There remains, naturally, the problem of *matter* of which some of these objects consisted.

ground on more than one point. The truth is that it hankered to give ground. Ten years ago, any symmetrical system whatsoever which gave the appearance of order – dialectical materialism, anti-Semitism, Nazism – was enough to fascinate men. Why not fall under the spell of Tlön and submit to the minute and vast evidence of an ordered planet? Useless to reply that reality, too, is ordered. It may be so, but in accordance with divine laws – I translate: inhuman laws – which we will never completely perceive. Tlön may be a labyrinth, but it is a labyrinth plotted by men, a labyrinth destined to be deciphered by men.

Contact with Tlön and the ways of Tlön have disintegrated this world. Captivated by its discipline, humanity forgets and goes on forgetting that it is the discipline of chess players, not of angels. Now, the conjectural 'primitive language' of Tlön has found its way into the schools. Now, the teaching of its harmonious history, full of stirring episodes, has obliterated the history which dominated my childhood. Now, in all memories, a fictitious past occupies the place of any other. We know nothing about it with any certainty, not even that it is false. Numismatics, pharmacology, and archaeology have been revised. I gather that biology and mathematics are awaiting their avatar. ... A scattered dynasty of solitaries has changed the face of the world. Its task continues. If our foresight is not mistaken, a hundred years from now someone will discover the hundred volumes of the *Second Encyclopaedia of Tlön*.

Then, English, French, and mere Spanish will disappear from this planet. The world will be Tlön. I take no notice. I go on revising, in the quiet of the days in the hotel at Androgué, a tentative translation into Spanish, in the style of Quevedo, which I do not intend to see published, of Sir Thomas Browne's *Urn Burial*.

Translated by ALASTAIR REID

THE APPROACH TO AL-MU'TASIM

Philip Guedalla writes that the novel *The Approach to Al-Mu'tasim* by the Bombay lawyer Mir Bahadur Ali 'is a rather uncomfortable combination of those allegorical poems of Islam which rarely fail to interest their translator and of those detective novels which inevitably surpass John H. Watson and refine the horror of human life found in the most irreproachable boarding houses of Brighton.' Previously, Mr Cecil Roberts had spoken harshly of Bahadur's book, condemning 'the double, improbable tutelage of Wilkie Collins and of Farid ud-din Attar, the illustrious twelfth-century Persian': a tranquil enough observation, which Guedalla repeats without notable emendation but in a choleric tone of voice. Essentially, both critics are in agreement: both indicate the detective story mechanism of the novel and its mystic undercurrent. This hybridization may cause us to imagine some likeness with Chesterton; we will soon see that there is no such thing.

The *edito princeps* of *The Approach to Al-Mu'tasim* appeared in Bombay toward the end of 1932. The paper used was almost the quality of newsprint; the cover proclaimed to the buyer that the book was the first detective novel written by a native of Bombay City. Within a few months the public bought up four printings of a thousand copies each. The *Bombay Quarterly Review*, the *Bombay Gazette*, the *Calcutta Review*, the *Hindustan Review* (of Allahabad), and the *Calcutta Englishman* distributed their eulogies. Thereupon Bahadur issued an illustrated edition of the book, which he now titled *The Conversation with the Man Called Al-Mu'tasim* and handsomely subtitled *A Game with Shifting Mirrors*. This is the edition which has just been reproduced and issued in London by Victor Gollancz, with a prologue by Dorothy L. Sayers, and the omission – perhaps merciful – of illustrations. I have it in front of me. The first edition, which I suspect is far superior, I have never succeeded in finding. I am authorized in this last judgement by an appendix which summarizes the fundamental difference between the primitive version of 1932 and the 1934 edition. Before examining the book – and arguing its merits – it would be well for me to indicate rapidly the general course of the work.

Its visible protagonist – we never learn his name – is a law student in Bombay. He disbelieves, blasphemously so, in the Islamic faith of his fathers. But at nightfall on the tenth night of the lunar month of Muharram, he finds himself in the centre of a civil tumult between Moslems and Hindus. The night is filled with drums and invocations: the great paper canopies of the Moslem procession force their way among the adverse multitude. A brick flung by a Hindu comes flying from a rooftop; someone sinks a dagger into another's belly; someone – Moslem? Hindu? – is killed and is stamped underfoot. Three thousand men battle: cane against revolver, obscenity against imprecation, God the Indivisible against the Gods. Aghast, the free-thinking student joins the fray. With desperate hands he kills (or thinks he kills) a Hindu. The Sirkar police – mounted, deafening-hooved, half asleep – intervene with their impartial lashes. Almost beneath the hooves of the horses, the student takes flight; he makes for the farthest outskirts of town. He crosses two sets of railroad tracks, or the same tracks twice. He scales the wall of an entangled garden, at the back of which rises a circular tower. 'A lean and evil mob of mooncoloured hounds' breaks out from behind the black rosebushes. Fiercely beset, he takes refuge in the tower. He climbs an iron ladder – some of the rungs are missing – and, once on the roof, where there is a blackish well in the centre, encounters a squalid man squatting by the light of the moon and urinating noisily. This man confides in him that his profession is to rob gold teeth from the white-shrouded cadavers which the Parsees leave in this tower. He talks of other equally vile matters and mentions that fourteen nights have passed since he last purified himself with buffalo dung. He speaks with manifest hatred of certain horse thieves in Guzerat, 'eaters of dogs and lizards, men as unclean as the two of us.' The sky begins to grow light: the air is filled with the low flight of fat vultures. Exhausted, the student falls asleep. When he awakes, the sun is high in the sky and the robber has disappeared. Also missing are a couple of Trichinopoly cigars and some silver rupees. In the face of the menaces foreshadowed by the previous night, the student resolves to lose himself in the depths of India. He meditates on how he has shown himself capable of killing an idolater, but not of knowing for certain whether a Moslem is more justified in his beliefs than a Hindu. He cannot get the name of Guzerat out of his mind, nor that of a certain *malka-sansi* (a woman of the robber caste) of Palanpur, the preferred target of curses and object of hatred for the despoiler of cadavers. He reasons that the rancour of a man so minutely vile is worthy of special eulogy. He resolves – with little hope – to look for the *malka-sansi*. After brief prayer, he sets forth on the long voyage with assured languor. Thus concludes the second chapter of the work.

It is impossible to trace the vicissitudes of the nineteen remaining chapters. There is a dizzy pullulation of *dramatis personæ*, not to speak of a biography which seems to exhaust the movements of the human spirit (ranging from infamy to mathematical speculation) or of a peregrination which encompasses the vast geography of Hindustan. The story which begins in Bombay continues in the lowlands of Palanpur, lingers an afternoon and a night at the stone gates of Bikaner, narrates the death of a blind astrologer in a Benares sewer, conspires in the multiform palace of Katmandu, prays and fornicates – amid the pestilential stench of Calcutta – in the Machua Bazaar, watches the days be born in the sea from an office in Madras, watches the afternoons die in the sea from a balcony in the state of Travancore, hesitates and kills at Indapur and closes its orbit of leagues and years in Bombay itself, a few paces away from the garden of the mooncoloured hounds.

The plot is as follows: a man, the incredulous and fugitive student whom we already know, falls among people of the vilest class and adjusts himself to them, in a kind of contest of infamy. All at once – with the miraculous consternation of Robinson Crusoe faced with the human footprint in the sand

– he perceives some mitigation in this infamy: a tenderness, an exaltation, a silence in one of the abhorrent men. 'It was as if a more complex interlocutor had joined the dialogue.' He knows that the vile man conversing with him is incapable of this momentaneous decorum; from this fact he concludes that the other, for the moment, is the reflection of a friend, or of the friend of a friend. Rethinking the problem he arrives at a mysterious conviction: some place in the world there is a man from whom this clarity emanates; some place in the world there is a man who is this clarity. The student resolves to dedicate his life to finding him.

The general argument is thus glimpsed: the insatiable search for a soul through the subtle reflections which this soul has left in others; in the beginning, the faint trace of a smile or of a word; in the end, diverse and increasing splendors of reason, of the imagination and of good. In the measure that the men questioned have known Al-Mu'tasim more intimately, in that measure is their divine portion the greater – though it is always clear that they are mere mirrors. Mathematical technicality is applicable: Bahadur's burdened novel is an ascending progression, whose final end is the presentiment of a 'man called Al-Mu'tasim.' The immediate antecedent of Al-Mu'tasim is a supremely happy and courteous Persian bookseller. The predecessor of this bookseller is a saint. . . .

After many years the student arrives at a gallery 'at the rear of which there is a door hung with a cheap and copiously beaded mat curtain; from behind it emanates a great radiance.' The student claps his hands once, twice, and asks for Al-Mu'tasim. A man's voice – the incredible voice of Al-Mu'tasim – urges him to come in. The student draws back the curtain and steps forward. The novel ends.

Unless I am deceived, the successful execution of such an argument imposes two obligations upon the writer: one, the various invention of prophetic traits; the other, the obligation of seeing to it that the hero prefigured by these traits be no mere convention or phantom. Bahadur satisfies the former; I do not know to what degree he satisfies the second. In other words: the extraordinary and unseen Al-Mu'tasim should give us the impression of a real character, not that of a jumble of insipid superlatives. In the 1932 version, the supernatural notes are scarce: 'the man named Al-Mu'tasim' is to some degree a symbol, but he does not lack idiosyncratic personal features. Unfortunately, this literary good conduct did not last long. In the 1934 version – which I have at hand – the novel sinks into allegory: Al-Mu'tasim is the emblem of God, and the punctual itinerary of the hero is in some manner the forward progress of the soul in its mystic ascent. Grievous details abound: a Negro Jew from Cochin speaking of Al-Mu'tasim says that his skin is dark; a Christian describes him standing atop a tower with his arms outspread; a Red lama remembers him seated 'like that image of yak lard which I modelled and adored in the monastery at Tashilhumpo.' These declarations are all meant to insinuate a unitary God who accommodates Himself to human diversities. To my mind, the idea is not very stimulating. I will not say the same of this other one: of the conjecture that the Almighty is also in search of Someone, and *that* Someone in search of some superior Someone (or merely indispensable or equal Someone), and thus on to the end – or better, the endlessness – of Time, or on and on in some cyclical form. Al-Mu'tasim (the name is the same as that of the eighth Abbasside, who was victor in eight battles, engendered eight male and eight female children, left behind eight thousand slaves and reigned during eight years, eight moons, and eight days) etymologically means *The Seeker of Shelter*. In the 1932 version, the fact that the object of the pilgrimage should be in turn a pilgrim opportunely justified the difficulty of finding him. In the 1934 version, it gives grounds to the extravagant theology I have mentioned. Mir Bahadur Ali is, as we have seen, incapable of evading the most vulgar of art's temptations: that of being a genius.

After rereading, I am apprehensive lest I have not sufficiently underlined the book's virtues. It contains some very civilized expressions: for example, a certain argument in the nineteenth chapter in which one feels a presentiment that one

of the antagonists is a friend of Al-Mu'tasim when he will not
refute the sophisms of his opponent 'so as not to be right in a
triumphal fashion.'

*

That a present-day book should derive from an ancient one is
clearly honourable: especially since no one (as Johnson says)
likes to be indebted to his contemporaries. The repeated, but
insignificant, contacts of Joyce's *Ulysses* with the Homeric
Odyssey continue to enjoy – I shall never know why – the
harebrained admiration of the critics. The coincidence in
Bahadur's novel with Farid ud-din Attar's venerated *Colloquy
of the Birds* are rewarded with the no less mysterious applause
of London, and even of Allahabad and Calcutta. Other
derivations for Bahadur's novel are not wanting. One inquisi-
tor has enumerated certain analogies in the novel's first scene
with elements from Kipling's story *On the City Wall*. Bahadur
has admitted the connection, but has alleged that it would be
most abnormal if two paintings depicting the tenth night of
Muharram did not coincide in some way. . . .

Eliot, with greater justice, recalls the seventy cantos of the
incomplete allegory *The Faërie Queene*, where the heroine,
Gloriana, does not appear a single time – as previously
pointed out in a censure by Richard William Church (*Spenser*,
1879). With all humility, I wish to mention a distant, and
possible, predecessor: the Jerusalem cabalist Isaac Luria, who
in the sixteenth century proclaimed that the soul of an
ancestor or that of a master might enter the soul of an
unfortunate to comfort or instruct him. *Ibbür* is the name for
this type of metempsychosis.*

1935   *Translated by* ANTHONY KERRIGAN

* I have referred, in the course of this note, to the *Mantiq ut-Tair* (*Colloquy
of the Birds*) by the Persian mystic Farid ud-din Abu Talib Mehammed ibn-
Ibrahim Attar, who was assassinated by the soldiers of Tului, Genghis
Khan's son, when Nishapur was sacked. Perhaps it will not prove idle to
summarize the poem. The faraway king of the birds, the Simurg, drops an
exquisite feather in the middle of China; weary of their ancient anarchy, the
birds determine to find it. They know that their king's name means 'Thirty

Birds'; they know that his royal palace stands on the Kaf, the circular mountain which surrounds the earth. They undertake the almost infinite adventure. They fly over seven valleys, or seven seas; the next-to-the-last one is called Vertigo; the last, Annihilation. Many of the pilgrims desert; others perish. Thirty of them, purified by their labours, set foot upon the Mountain of the Simurg. At last they contemplate it: they perceive that *they* are the Simurg, and that the Simurg is each one of them and all of them. The *Enneads* of Plotinus, too, declare – v, 8, 4 – a paradisiacal extension of the principle of identity: 'Everything in the intelligible heaven is everywhere. Anything is all things. The sun is all the stars, and each star is all stars and the sun.' The *Mantiq ut-Tair* has been translated into French by Garcin de Tassy, into English by Edward Fitzgerald. For purposes of this note I have consulted the tenth volume of Burton's *The Thousand and One Nights* and the monograph titled *The Persian Mystics: Attar* (1932) by Margaret Smith.

The points of contact between this poem and Mir Bahadur's novel are not over-numerous. In Chapter 20, certain words attributed by a Persian bookseller to Al-Mu'tasim are, perhaps, a magnification of certain others spoken by the hero. This ambiguous analogy and others like it may merely signify the identification of the searcher with the sought; they also might mean that the latter influences the former. Another chapter insinuates that Al-Mu'tasim is the 'Hindu' whom the student believes he has killed.

PIERRE MENARD, AUTHOR OF DON QUIXOTE

To Silvina Ocampo

The *visible* works left by this novelist are easily and briefly enumerated. It is therefore impossible to forgive the omissions and additions perpetrated by Madame Henri Bachelier in a fallacious catalogue that a certain newspaper, whose Protestant tendencies are no secret, was inconsiderate enough to inflict on its wretched readers – even though they are few and Calvinist, if not Masonic and circumcised. Menard's true friends regarded this catalogue with alarm, and even with a certain sadness. It is as if yesterday we were gathered together before the final marble and the fateful cypresses, and already Error is trying to tarnish his Memory. ... Decidedly, a brief rectification is inevitable.

I am certain that it would be very easy to challenge my meagre authority. I hope, nevertheless, that I will not be prevented from mentioning two important testimonials. The Baroness de Bacourt (at whose unforgettable *vendredis* I had the honour of becoming acquainted with the late lamented poet) has seen fit to approve these lines. The Countess de Bagnoregio, one of the most refined minds in the Principality of Monaco (and now of Pittsburgh, Pennsylvania, since her recent marriage to the international philanthropist Simon Kautsch who, alas, has been so slandered by the victims of his disinterested handiwork), has sacrificed to 'truth and death' (those are her words) that majestic reserve which distinguishes her, and in an open letter published in the magazine *Luxe* also grants me her consent. These authorizations, I believe, are not insufficient.

I have said that Menard's *visible* lifework is easily enumerated. Having carefully examined his private archives, I have been able to verify that it consists of the following:

(a) A symbolist sonnet which appeared twice (with variations) in the magazine *La Conque* (the March and October issues of 1899).

(b) A monograph on the possibility of constructing a poetic vocabulary of concepts that would not be synonyms or periphrases of those which make up ordinary language, 'but ideal objects created by means of common agreement and destined essentially to fill poetic needs' (Nîmes, 1901).

(c) A monograph on 'certain connections or affinities' among the ideas of Descartes, Leibnitz and John Wilkins (Nîmes, 1903).

(d) A monograph on the *Characteristica Universalis* of Leibnitz (Nîmes, 1904).

(e) A technical article on the possibility of enriching the game of chess by means of eliminating one of the rooks' pawns. Menard proposes, recommends, disputes, and ends by rejecting this innovation.

(f) A monograph on the *Ars Magna Generalis* of Ramón Lull (Nîmes, 1906).

(g) A translation with prologue and notes of the *Libro de la invención y arte del juego del axedrez* by Ruy López de Segura (Paris, 1907).

(h) The rough draft of a monograph on the symbolic logic of George Boole.

(i) An examination of the metric laws essential to French prose, illustrated with examples from Saint-Simon (*Revue des langues romanes*, Montpellier, October, 1909).

(j) An answer to Luc Durtain (who had denied the existence of such laws) illustrated with examples from Luc Durtain (*Revue des langues romanes*, Montpellier, December, 1909).

(k) A manuscript translation of the *Aguja de navegar cultos* of Quevedo, entitled *La boussole des précieux*.

(l) A preface to the catalogue of the exposition of lithographs by Carolus Hourcade (Nîmes, 1914).

(m) His work, *Les problèmes d'un problème* (Paris, 1917), which takes up in chronological order the various solutions of the famous problem of Achilles and the tortoise. Two editions of this book have appeared so far; the second has as an epigraph Leibnitz' advice 'Ne craignez point, monsieur, la tortue,' and contains revisions of the chapters dedicated to Russell and Descartes.

(n) An obstinate analysis of the 'syntactic habits' of Toulet (*N.R.F.*, March, 1921). I remember that Menard used to declare that censuring and praising were sentimental operations which had nothing to do with criticism.

(o) A transposition into Alexandrines of *Le Cimetière marin* of Paul Valéry (*N.R.F.*, January, 1928).

(p) An invective against Paul Valéry in the *Journal for the Suppression of Reality* of Jacques Reboul. (This invective, it should be stated parenthetically, is the exact reverse of his true opinion of Valéry. The latter understood it as such, and the old friendship between the two was never endangered.)

(q) A 'definition' of the Countess of Bagnoregio in the 'victorious volume' – the phrase is that of another collaborator, Gabriele d'Annunzio – which this lady publishes yearly to rectify the inevitable falsifications of journalism and to present 'to the world and to Italy' an authentic effigy of her person, which is so exposed (by reason of her beauty and her activities) to erroneous or hasty interpretations.

(r) A cycle of admirable sonnets for the Baroness de Bacourt (1934).

(s) A manuscript list of verses which owe their effectiveness to punctuation.*

Up to this point (with no other omission than that of some vague, circumstantial sonnets for the hospitable, or greedy, album of Madame Henri Bachelier) we have the *visible* part of Menard's works in chronological order. Now I will pass over to that other part, which is subterranean, interminably heroic, and unequalled, and which is also – oh, the possibilities inherent in the man! – inconclusive. This work, possibly the most significant of our time, consists of the ninth and thirty-

---

* Madame Henri Bachelier also lists a literal translation of a literal translation done by Quevedo of the *Introduction à la vie dévote* of Saint Francis of Sales. In Pierre Menard's library there are no traces of such a work. She must have misunderstood a remark of his which he had intended as a joke.

eighth chapters of Part One of *Don Quixote* and a fragment of
the twenty-second chapter. I realize that such an affirmation
seems absurd; but the justification of this 'absurdity' is the
primary object of this note.*

Two texts of unequal value inspired the undertaking. One
was that philological fragment of Novalis – No. 2005 of the
Dresden edition – which outlines the theme of *total* identification with a specific author. The other was one of those
parasitic books which places Christ on a boulevard, Hamlet
on the Cannebière and Don Quixote on Wall Street. Like any
man of good taste, Menard detested these useless carnivals,
only suitable – he used to say – for evoking plebeian delight in
anachronism, or (what is worse) charming us with the
primary idea that all epochs are the same, or that they are
different. He considered more interesting, even though it had
been carried out in a contradictory and superficial way,
Daudet's famous plan: to unite, in *one* figure, Tartarin, the
Ingenious Gentleman and his squire. ... Any insinuation
that Menard dedicated his life to the writing of a contemporary *Don Quixote* is a calumny of his illustrious memory.

He did not want to compose another *Don Quixote* – which
would be so easy – but *the Don Quixote*. It is unnecessary to
add that his aim was never to produce a mechanical transcription of the original; he did not propose to copy it. His
admirable ambition was to produce pages which would
coincide – word for word and line for line – with those of
Miguel de Cervantes.

'My intent is merely astonishing,' he wrote me from
Bayonne on 30 December, 1934. 'The ultimate goal of a
theological or metaphysical demonstration – the external
world, God, chance, universal forms – is no less anterior or
common than this novel which I am now developing. The
only difference is that philosophers publish in pleasant

---

* I also had another, secondary intent – that of sketching a portrait of
Pierre Menard. But how would I dare to compete with the golden pages the
Baroness de Bacourt tells me she is preparing, or with the delicate and
precise pencil of Carolus Hourcade?

volumes the intermediary stages of their work and that I have decided to lose them.' And, in fact, not one page of a rough draft remains to bear witness to this work of years.

The initial method he conceived was relatively simple: to know Spanish well, to re-embrace the Catholic faith, to fight against Moors and Turks, to forget European history between 1602 and 1918, and to *be* Miguel de Cervantes. Pierre Menard studied this procedure (I know that he arrived at a rather faithful handling of seventeenth-century Spanish) but rejected it as too easy. Rather because it was impossible, the reader will say! I agree, but the undertaking was impossible from the start, and of all the possible means of carrying it out, this one was the least interesting. To be, in the twentieth century, a popular novelist of the seventeenth seemed to him a diminution. To be, in some way, Cervantes and to arrive at *Don Quixote* seemed to him less arduous – and consequently less interesting – than to continue being Pierre Menard and to arrive at *Don Quixote* through the experiences of Pierre Menard. (This conviction, let it be said in passing, forced him to exclude the autobiographical prologue of the second part of *Don Quixote*. To include this prologue would have meant creating another personage – Cervantes – but it would also have meant presenting *Don Quixote* as the work of this personage and not of Menard. He naturally denied himself such an easy solution.) 'My undertaking is not essentially difficult,' I read in another part of the same letter. 'I would only have to be immortal in order to carry it out.' Shall I confess that I often imagine that he finished it and that I am reading *Don Quixote* – the entire work – as if Menard had conceived it? Several nights ago, while leafing through Chapter XXVI – which he had never attempted – I recognized our friend's style and, as it were, his voice in this exceptional phrase: *the nymphs of the rivers, mournful and humid Echo.* This effective combination of two adjectives, one moral and the other physical, reminded me of a line from Shakespeare which we discussed one afternoon:

Where a malignant and turbaned Turk . . .

Why precisely *Don Quixote*, our reader will ask. Such a preference would not have been inexplicable in a Spaniard; but it undoubtedly was in a symbolist from Nîmes, essentially devoted to Poe, who engendered Baudelaire, who engendered Mallarmé, who engendered Valéry, who engendered Edmond Teste. The letter quoted above clarifies this point. '*Don Quixote*,' Menard explains, 'interests me profoundly, but it does not seem to me to have been – how shall I say it – inevitable. I cannot imagine the universe without the interjection of Edgar Allan Poe

Ah, bear in mind this garden was enchanted!

or without the *Bateau ivre* or the *Ancient Mariner*, but I know that I am capable of imagining it without *Don Quixote*. (I speak, naturally, of my personal capacity, not of the historical repercussions of these works.) *Don Quixote* is an accidental book, *Don Quixote* is unnecessary. I can premeditate writing, I can write it, without incurring a tautology. When I was twelve or thirteen years old I read it, perhaps in its entirety. Since then I have reread several chapters attentively, but not the ones I am going to undertake. I have likewise studied the *entremeses*, the comedies, the *Galatea*, the exemplary novels, and the undoubtedly laborious efforts of *Pésiles y Sigismunda* and the *Viaje al Parnaso*. ... My general memory of *Don Quixote*, simplified by forgetfulness and indifference, is much the same as the imprecise, anterior image of a book not yet written. Once this image (which no one can deny me in good faith) has been postulated, my problems are undeniably considerably more difficult than those which Cervantes faced. My affable precursor did not refuse the collaboration of fate; he went along composing his immortal work a little *à la diable*, swept along by inertias of language and invention. I have contracted the mysterious duty of reconstructing literally his spontaneous work. My solitary game is governed by two polar laws. The first permits me to attempt variants of a formal and psychological nature; the second obliges me to sacrifice them to the "original" text and irrefutably to rationalize this annihilation. .... To these artificial obstacles one must add another congenital one. To compose *Don Quixote* at the beginning of the seventeenth century was a reasonable, necessary and perhaps inevitable undertaking; at the beginning of the twentieth century it is almost impossible. It is not in vain that three hundred years have passed, charged with the most complex happenings – among them, to mention only one, that same *Don Quixote*.'

In spite of these three obstacles, the fragmentary *Don Quixote* of Menard is more subtle than that of Cervantes. The latter indulges in a rather coarse opposition between tales of knighthood and the meagre, provincial reality of his country; Menard chooses as 'reality' the land of Carmen during the century of Lepanto and Lope. What Hispanophile would not have advised Maurice Barrès or Dr Rodríguez Larreta to make such a choice! Menard, as if it were the most natural thing in the world, eludes them. In his work there are neither bands of gypsies, conquistadors, mystics, Philip the Seconds, nor autos-da-fé. He disregards or proscribes local colour. This disdain indicates a new approach to the historical novel. This disdain condemns *Salammbô* without appeal.

It is no less astonishing to consider isolated chapters. Let us examine, for instance, Chapter XXXVIII of Part One 'which treats of the curious discourse that Don Quixote delivered on the subject of arms and letters.' As is known, Don Quixote (like Quevedo in a later, analogous passage of *La hora de todos*) passes judgement against letters and in favour of arms. Cervantes was an old soldier, which explains such a judgement. But that the *Don Quixote* of Pierre Menard – a contemporary of *La trahison des clercs* and Bertrand Russell – should relapse into these nebulous sophistries! Madame Bachelier has seen in them an admirable and typical subordination of the author to the psychology of the hero; others (by no means perspicaciously) a *transcription* of *Don Quixote*; the Baroness de Bacourt, the influence of Nietzsche. To this third interpretation (which seems to me irrefutable) I do not know if I would dare to add a fourth, which coincides very well with the divine modesty of Pierre Menard: his resigned or ironic

habit of propounding ideas which were the strict reverse of
those he preferred. (One will remember his diatribe against
Paul Valéry in the ephemeral journal of the superrealist
Jacques Reboul.) The text of Cervantes and that of Menard
are verbally identical, but the second is almost infinitely
richer. (More ambiguous, his detractors will say; but ambi-
guity is a richness.) It is a revelation to compare the *Don
Quixote* of Menard with that of Cervantes. The latter, for
instance, wrote (*Don Quixote*, Part One, Chapter Nine):

*. . . la verdad, cuya madre es la historia, émula del tiempo, depósito
de las acciones, testigo de lo pasado, ejemplo y aviso de lo presente,
advertencia de lo por venir.*
[. . . truth, whose mother is history, who is the rival of time,
depository of deeds, witness of the past, example and lesson to
the present, and warning to the future.]

Written in the seventeenth century, written by the
'ingenious layman' Cervantes, this enumeration is a mere
rhetorical eulogy of history. Menard, on the other hand,
writes:

*. . . la verdad, cuya madre es la historia, émula del tiempo, depósito
de las acciones, testigo de lo pasado, ejemplo y aviso de lo presente,
advertencia de lo por venir.*
[. . . truth, whose mother is history, who is the rival of time,
depository of deeds, witness of the past, example and lesson to
the present, and warning to the future.]

History, *mother* of truth; the idea is astounding. Menard, a
contemporary of William James, does not define history as an
investigation of reality, but as its origin. Historical truth, for
him, is not what took place; it is what we think took place.
The final clauses – *example and lesson to the present, and warning
to the future* – are shamelessly pragmatic.

Equally vivid is the contrast in styles. The archaic style of
Menard – in the last analysis, a foreigner – suffers from a
certain affectation. Not so that of his precursor, who handles
easily the ordinary Spanish of his time.

There is no intellectual exercise which is not ultimately useless. A philosophical doctrine is in the beginning a seemingly true description of the universe; as the years pass it becomes a mere chapter – if not a paragraph or a noun – in the history of philosophy. In literature, this ultimate decay is even more notorious. '*Don Quixote*,' Menard once told me, 'was above all an agreeable book; now it is an occasion for patriotic toasts, grammatical arrogance and obscene de-luxe editions. Glory is an incomprehension, and perhaps the worst.'

The nihilist arguments contain nothing new; what is unusual is the decision Pierre Menard derived from them. He resolved to outstrip that vanity which awaits all the woes of mankind; he undertook a task that was complex in the extreme and futile from the outset. He dedicated his conscience and nightly studies to the repetition of a pre-existing book in a foreign tongue. The number of rough drafts kept on increasing; he tenaciously made corrections and tore up thousands of manuscript pages.* He did not permit them to be examined, and he took great care that they would not survive him. It is in vain that I have tried to reconstruct them.

I have thought that it is legitimate to consider the 'final' *Don Quixote* as a kind of palimpsest, in which should appear traces – tenuous but not undecipherable – of the 'previous' handwriting of our friend. Unfortunately, only a second Pierre Menard, inverting the work of the former, could exhume and resuscitate these Troys. . . .

'To think, analyse and invent,' he also wrote me, 'are not anomalous acts, but the normal respiration of the intelligence. To glorify the occasional fulfillment of this function, to treasure ancient thoughts of others, to remember with incredulous amazement that the *doctor universalis* thought, is to confess our languor or barbarism. Every man should be capable of all ideas, and I believe that in the future he will be.'

* I remember his square-ruled notebooks, the black streaks where he had crossed out words, his peculiar typographical symbols and his insect-like handwriting. In the late afternoon he liked to go for walks on the outskirts of Nîmes; he would take a notebook with him and make a gay bonfire.

Menard (perhaps without wishing to) has enriched, by means of a new technique, the hesitant and rudimentary art of reading: the technique is one of deliberate anachronism and erroneous attributions. This technique, with its infinite applications, urges us to run through the *Odyssey* as if it were written after the *Aeneid*, and to read *Le jardin du Centaure* by Madame Henri Bachelier as if it were by Madame Henri Bachelier. This technique would fill the dullest books with adventure. Would not the attributing of *The Imitation of Christ* to Louis Ferdinand Céline or James Joyce be a sufficient renovation of its tenuous spiritual counsels?

Nîmes
1939   *Translated by* ANTHONY BONNER

THE CIRCULAR RUINS

And if he left off dreaming about you ...
Through the Looking Glass, VI.

No one saw him disembark in the unanimous night, no one saw the bamboo canoe sink into the sacred mud, but in a few days there was no one who did not know that the taciturn man came from the South and that his home had been one of those numberless villages upstream in the deeply cleft side of the mountain, where the Zend language has not been contaminated by Greek and where leprosy is infrequent. What is certain is that the grey man kissed the mud, climbed up the bank without pushing aside (probably, without feeling) the blades which were lacerating his flesh, and crawled, nauseated and bloodstained, up to the circular enclosure crowned with a stone tiger or horse, which sometimes was the colour of flame and now was that of ashes. This circle was a temple which had been devoured by ancient fires, profaned by the miasmal jungle, and whose god no longer received the homage of men. The stranger stretched himself out beneath the pedestal. He was awakened by the sun high overhead. He was not astonished to find that his wounds had healed; he closed his pallid eyes and slept, not through weakness of flesh but through determination of will. He knew that this temple was the place required for his invincible intent; he knew that the incessant trees had not succeeded in strangling the ruins of another propitious temple downstream which had once belonged to gods now burned and dead; he knew that his immediate obligation was to dream. Towards midnight he was awakened by the inconsolable shriek of a bird. Tracks of bare feet, some figs and a jug warned him that the men of the region had been spying respectfully on his sleep, soliciting his protection or afraid of his magic. He felt a chill of fear, and sought out a sepulchral niche in the dilapidated wall where he concealed himself among unfamiliar leaves.

The purpose which guided him was not impossible, though supernatural. He wanted to dream a man; he wanted to dream him in minute entirety and impose him on reality. This magic project had exhausted the entire expanse of his mind; if someone had asked him his name or to relate some event of his former life, he would not have been able to give an answer. This uninhabited, ruined temple suited him, for it contained a minimum of visible world; the proximity of the workmen also suited him, for they took it upon themselves to provide for his frugal needs. The rice and fruit they brought him were nourishment enough for his body, which was consecrated to the sole task of sleeping and dreaming.

At first, his dreams were chaotic; then in a short while they became dialectic in nature. The stranger dreamed that he was in the centre of a circular amphitheatre which was more or less the burnt temple; clouds of taciturn students filled the tiers of seats; the faces of the farthest ones hung at a distance of many centuries and as high as the stars, but their features were completely precise. The man lectured his pupils on anatomy, cosmography, and magic: the faces listened anxiously and tried to answer understandingly, as if they guessed the importance of that examination which would redeem one of them from his condition of empty illusion and interpolate him into the real world. Asleep or awake, the man thought over the answers of his phantoms, did not allow himself to be deceived by impostors, and in certain perplexities he sensed a growing intelligence. He was seeking a soul worthy of participating in the universe.

After nine or ten nights he understood with a certain bitterness that he could expect nothing from those pupils who accepted his doctrine passively, but that he could expect something from those who occasionally dared to oppose him. The former group, although worthy of love and affection, could not ascend to the level of individuals; the latter pre-existed to a slightly greater degree. One afternoon (now afternoons were also given over to sleep, now he was only awake for a couple of hours at daybreak) he dismissed the vast illusory student body for good and kept only one pupil. He was a taciturn, sallow boy, at times intractable, and whose sharp features resembled those of his dreamer. The brusque elimination of his fellow students did not disconcert him for long; after a few private lessons, his progress was enough to astound the teacher, Nevertheless, a catastrophe took place. One day, the man emerged from his sleep as if from a viscous desert, looked at the useless afternoon light which he immediately confused with the dawn, and understood that he had not dreamed. All that night and all day long, the intolerable lucidity of insomnia fell upon him. He tried exploring the forest, to lose his strength; among the hemlock he barely succeeded in experiencing several short snatches of sleep, veined with fleeting, rudimentary visions that were useless. He tried to assemble the student body but scarcely had he articulated a few brief words of exhortation when it became deformed and was then erased. In his almost perpetual vigil, tears of anger burned his old eyes.

He understood that modelling the incoherent and vertiginous matter of which dreams are composed was the most difficult task that a man could undertake, even though he should penetrate all the enigmas of a superior and inferior order; much more difficult than weaving a rope out of sand or coining the faceless wind. He swore he would forget the enormous hallucination which had thrown him off at first, and he sought another method of work. Before putting it into execution, he spent a month recovering his strength, which had been squandered by his delirium. He abandoned all premeditation of dreaming and almost immediately succeeded in sleeping a reasonable part of each day. The few times that he had dreams during this period, he paid no attention to them. Before resuming his task, he waited until the moon's disk was perfect. Then, in the afternoon, he purified himself in the waters of the river, worshipped the planetary gods, pronounced the prescribed syllables of a mighty name, and went to sleep. He dreamed almost immediately, with his heart throbbing.

He dreamed that it was warm, secret, about the size of a clenched fist, and of a garnet colour within the penumbra of a human body as yet without face or sex; during fourteen lucid nights he dreamt of it with meticulous love. Every night he perceived it more clearly. He did not touch it; he only permitted himself to witness it, to observe it, and occasionally to rectify it with a glance. He perceived it and lived it from all angles and distances. On the fourteenth night he lightly touched the pulmonary artery with his index finger, then the whole heart, outside and inside. He was satisfied with the examination. He deliberately did not dream for a night; he then took up the heart again, invoked the name of a planet, and undertook the vision of another of the principal organs. Within a year he had come to the skeleton and the eyelids. The innumerable hair was perhaps the most difficult task. He dreamed an entire man – a young man, but who did not sit up or talk, who was unable to open his eyes. Night after night, the man dreamt him asleep.

In the Gnostic cosmogonies, demiurges fashion a red Adam who cannot stand; as clumsy, crude and elemental as this Adam of dust was the Adam of dreams forged by the wizard's nights. One afternoon, the man almost destroyed his entire work, but then changed his mind. (It would have been better had he destroyed it.) When he had exhausted all supplications to the deities of the earth, he threw himself at the feet of the effigy which was perhaps a tiger or perhaps a colt and implored its unknown help. That evening, at twilight, he dreamt of the statue. He dreamt it was alive, tremulous: it was not an atrocious bastard of a tiger and a colt, but at the same time these two fiery creatures and also a bull, a rose, and a storm. This multiple god revealed to him that his earthly name was Fire, and that in this circular temple (and in others like it) people had once made sacrifices to him and worshipped him, and that he would magically animate the dreamed phantom, in such a way that all creatures, except Fire itself and the dreamer, would believe it to be a man of flesh and blood. He commanded that once this man had been instructed in all the rites, he should be sent to the other ruined temple whose pyramids were still standing downstream, so that some voice would glorify him in that deserted edifice. In the dream of the man that dreamed, the dreamed one woke.

The wizard carried out the orders he had been given. He devoted a certain length of time (which finally proved to be two years) to instructing him in the mysteries of the universe and the cult of fire. Secretly, he was pained at the idea of being separated from him. On the pretext of pedagogical necessity, each day he increased the number of hours dedicated to dreaming. He also remade the right shoulder, which was somewhat defective. At times, he was disturbed by the impression that all this had already happened. . . . In general, his days were happy; when he closed his eyes, he thought: *Now I will be with my son.* Or more rarely: *The son I have engendered is waiting for me and will not exist if I do not go to him.*

Gradually, he began accustoming him to reality. Once he ordered him to place a flag on a faraway peak. The next day the flag was fluttering on the peak. He tried other analogous experiments, each time more audacious. With a certain bitterness, he understood that his son was ready to be born – and perhaps impatient. That night he kissed him for the first time and sent him off to the other temple whose remains were turning white downstream, across many miles of inextricable jungle and marshes. Before doing this (and so that his son should never know that he was a phantom, so that he should think himself a man like any other) he destroyed in him all memory of his years of apprenticeship.

His victory and peace became blurred with boredom. In the twilight times of dusk and dawn, he would prostrate himself before the stone figure, perhaps imagining his unreal son carrying out identical rites in other circular ruins downstream; at night he no longer dreamed, or dreamed as any man does. His perceptions of the sounds and forms of the universe became somewhat pallid: his absent son was being nourished by these diminutions of his soul. The purpose of his life had been fulfilled; the man remained in a kind of ecstasy. After a certain time, which some chroniclers prefer to compute in years and others in decades, two oarsmen awoke him at midnight; he could not see their faces, but they spoke to him of a charmed man in a temple of the North, capable of walking on fire without burning himself. The wizard suddenly remembered the words of the god. He remembered that of all the creatures that people the earth, Fire was the only one who knew his son to be a phantom. This memory, which at first calmed him, ended by tormenting him. He feared lest his son should meditate on this abnormal privilege and by some means find out he was a mere simulacrum. Not to be a man, to be a projection of another man's dreams – what an incomparable humiliation, what madness! Any father is interested in the sons he has procreated (or permitted) out of the mere confusion of happiness; it was natural that the wizard should fear for the future of that son whom he had thought out entrail by entrail, feature by feature, in a thousand and one secret nights.

His misgivings ended abruptly, but not without certain forewarnings. First (after a long drought) a remote cloud, as light as a bird, appeared on a hill; then, towards the South, the sky took on the rose colour of leopard's gums; then came clouds of smoke which rusted the metal of the nights; afterwards came the panic-stricken flight of wild animals. For what had happened many centuries before was repeating itself. The ruins of the sanctuary of the god of Fire was destroyed by fire. In a dawn without birds, the wizard saw the concentric fire licking the walls. For a moment, he thought of taking refuge in the water, but then he understood that death was coming to crown his old age and absolve him from his labours. He walked towards the sheets of flame. They did not bite his flesh, they caressed him and flooded him without heat or combustion. With relief, with humiliation, with terror, he understood that he also was an illusion, that someone else was dreaming him.

Translated by ANTHONY BONNER

THE BABYLON LOTTERY

Like all men in Babylon I have been a proconsul; like all, a slave; I have also known omnipotence, opprobrium, jail. Look: the index finger of my right hand is missing. Look again: through this rent in my cape you can see a ruddy tattoo on my belly. It is the second symbol, Beth. This letter, on nights of full moon, gives me power over men whose mark is Ghimel; but it also subordinates me to those marked Aleph, who on moonless nights owe obedience to those marked Ghimel. In a cellar at dawn, I have severed the jugular vein of sacred bulls against a black rock. During one lunar year, I have been declared invisible: I shrieked and was not heard, I stole my bread and was not decapitated. I have known what the Greeks did not: uncertainty. In a bronze chamber, faced with the silent handkerchief of a strangler, hope has been faithful to me; in the river of delights, panic has not failed me. Heraclitus of Pontica admiringly relates that Pythagoras recalled having been Pyrrho, and before that Euphorbus, and before that some other mortal. In order to recall analogous vicissitudes I do not need to have recourse to death, nor even to imposture.

I owe this almost atrocious variety to an institution which other republics know nothing about, or which operates among them imperfectly and in secret: the lottery. I have not delved into its history; I do know that the wizards have been unable to come to any agreement; of its powerful designs I know what a man not versed in astrology might know of the moon. I come from a vertiginous country where the lottery forms a principal part of reality; until this very day I have thought about all this as little as I have about the behaviour of the indecipherable gods or about the beating of my own heart. Now, far from Babylon and its beloved customs, I think of the lottery with some astonishment and ponder the blasphemous conjectures murmured by men in the shadows at twilight.

My father related that anciently – a matter of centuries; of years? – the lottery in Babylon was a game of plebeian character. He said (I do not know with what degree of truth) that barbers gave rectangular bits of bone or decorated parchment in exchange for copper coins. A drawing of the lottery was held in the middle of the day: the winners received, without further corroboration from chance, silver-minted coins. The procedure, as you see, was elemental.

Naturally, these 'lotteries' failed. Their moral virtue was nil. They did not appeal to all the faculties of men: only to their hope. In the face of public indifference, the merchants who established these venal lotteries began to lose money. Someone attempted to introduce a slight reform: the interpolation of a certain small number of adverse outcomes among the favoured numbers. By means of this reform, the purchasers of numbered rectangles stood the double chance of winning a sum or of paying a fine often considerable in size. This slight danger – for each thirty favoured numbers there would be one adverse number – awoke, as was only natural, the public's interest. The Babylonians gave themselves up to the game. Anyone who did not acquire lots was looked upon as pusillanimous, mean-spirited. In time, this disdain multiplied. The person who did not play was despised, but the losers who paid the fine were also scorned. The Company (thus it began to be known at that time) was forced to take measures to protect the winners, who could not collect their prizes unless nearly the entire amount of the fines was already collected. The Company brought suit against the losers: the judge condemned them to pay the original fine plus costs or to spend a number of days in jail. Every loser chose jail, so as to defraud the Company. It was from this initial bravado of a few men that the all-powerful position of the Company – its ecclesiastical, metaphysical strength – was derived.

A short while later, the reports on the drawings omitted any enumeration of fines and limited themselves to publishing the jail sentences corresponding to each adverse number. This laconism, almost unnoticed at the time, became of capital importance. *It constituted the first appearance in the lottery of non-pecuniary elements.* Its success was great. Pushed

to such a measure by the players, the Company found itself
forced to increase its adverse numbers.

No one can deny that the people of Babylonia are highly
devoted to logic, even to symmetry. It struck them as
incoherent that the fortunate numbers should be computed in
round figures of money while the unfortunate should be
figured in terms of days and nights in jail. Some moralists
argued that the possession of money does not determine
happiness and that other forms of fortune are perhaps more
immediate.

There was another source of restlessness in the lower
depths. The members of the sacerdotal college multiplied the
stakes and plumbed the vicissitudes of terror and hope; the
poor, with reasonable or inevitable envy, saw themselves
excluded from this notoriously delicious exhilaration. The
just anxiety of all, poor and rich alike, to participate equally in
the lottery, inspired an indignant agitation, the memory of
which the years have not erased. Certain obstinate souls did
not comprehend, or pretended not to comprehend, that a new
order had come, a necessary historical stage. ... A slave stole
a crimson ticket, a ticket which earned him the right to have
his tongue burned in the next drawing. The criminal code
fixed the same penalty for the theft of a ticket. A number of
Babylonians argued that he deserved a red-hot poker by
virtue of the theft; others, more magnanimous, held that the
public executioner should apply the penalty of the lottery,
since chance had so determined. ...

Disturbances broke out, there was a lamentable shedding
of blood; but the people of Babylon imposed their will at last,
over the opposition of the rich. That is: the people fully
achieved their magnanimous ends. In the first place, it made
the Company accept complete public power. (This unifica-
tion was necessary, given the vastness and complexity of the
new operations.) In the second place, it forced the lottery to
be secret, free, and general. The sale of tickets for money was
abolished. Once initiated into the mysteries of Bel, every free
man automatically participated in the sacred drawings of lots,
which were carried out in the labyrinths of the gods every

seventy nights and which determined every man's fate until
the next exercise. The consequences were incalculable. A
happy drawing might motivate his elevation to the council of
wizards or his condemnation to the custody of an enemy
(notorious or intimate), or to find, in the peaceful shadows of
a room, the woman who had begun to disquiet him or whom
he had never expected to see again. An adverse drawing might
mean mutilation, a varied infamy, death. Sometimes a single
event – the tavern killing of C, the mysterious glorification of
B – might be the brilliant result of thirty or forty drawings.
But it must be recalled that the individuals of the Company
were (and are) all-powerful and astute as well. In many cases,
the knowledge that certain joys were the simple doing of
chance might have detracted from their excellence; to avoid
this inconvenience the Company's agents made use of suggestion and magic. Their moves, their management, were secret.
In the investigation of people's intimate hopes and intimate
terrors, they made use of astrologers and spies. There were
certain stone lions, there was a sacred privy called Qaphqa,
there were fissures in a dusty aqueduct which, according to
general opinion, *led to the Company*; malign or benevolent
people deposited accusations in these cracks. The denuncia-
tions were incorporated into an alphabetical archive of vari-
able veracity.

Incredibly enough, there were still complaints. The Company, with its habitual discretion, did not reply directly. It
preferred to scribble a brief argument – which now figures
among sacred scriptures – in the debris of a mask factory.
That doctrinal piece of literature observed that the lottery is
an interpolation of chance into the order of the world and that
to accept errors is not to contradict fate but merely to
corroborate it. It also observed that those lions and that
sacred recipient, though not unauthorized by the Company
(which did not renounce the right to consult them), func-
tioned without official guaranty.

This declaration pacified the public unease. It also produced other effects, not foreseen by the author. It deeply
modified the spirit and operations of the Company. (I have

little time left to tell what I know; we have been warned that the ship is ready to sail; but I will attempt to explain it.)

Improbable as it may be, no one had until then attempted to set up a general theory of games. A Babylonian is not highly speculative. He reveres the judgements of fate, he hands his life over to them, he places his hopes, his panic terror in them, but it never occurs to him to investigate their labyrinthian laws nor the giratory spheres which disclose them. Nevertheless, the unofficial declaration which I have mentioned inspired many discussions of a juridico-mathematical nature. From one of these discussions was born the following conjecture: if the lottery is an intensification of chance, a periodic infusion of chaos into the cosmos, would it not be desirable for chance to intervene at all stages of the lottery and not merely in the drawing? Is it not ridiculous for chance to dictate the death of someone, while the circumstances of his death – its silent reserve or publicity, the time limit of one hour or one century – should remain immune to hazard? These eminently just scruples finally provoked a considerable reform, whose complexities (intensified by the practice of centuries) are not understood except by a handful of specialists, but which I will attempt to summarize, even if only in a symbolic manner.

Let us imagine a first drawing, which eventuates in a sentence of death against some individual. To carry out the sentence, another drawing is set up, and this drawing proposes (let us say) nine possible executioners. Of these executioners, four can initiate a third drawing which will reveal the name of the actual executioner, two others can replace the adverse order with a fortunate order (the finding of a treasure, let us say), another may exacerbate the death sentence (that is: make it infamous or enrich it with torture), still others may refuse to carry it out. . . .

Such is the symbolic scheme. In reality, *the number of drawings is infinite*. No decision is final, all diverge into others. The ignorant suppose that an infinite number of drawings require an infinite amount of time; in reality, it is quite enough that time be infinitely subdivisible, as is the case in the famous parable of the Tortoise and the Hare. This infinitude harmonizes in an admirable manner with the sinuous numbers of Chance and of the Celestial Archetype of the Lottery adored by the Platonists. ...

A certain distorted echo of our ritual seems to have resounded along the Tiber: Aelius Lampridius, in his *Life of Antoninus Heliogabalus*, tells of how this emperor wrote down the lot of his guests on seashells, so that one would receive ten pounds of gold and another ten flies, ten dormice, ten bears. It is only right to remark that Heliogabalus was educated in Asia Minor, among the priests of the eponymous god.

There are also impersonal drawings, of undefined purpose: one drawing will decree that a sapphire from Taprobane be thrown into the waters of the Euphrates; another, that a bird be released from a tower roof; another, that a grain of sand be withdrawn (or added) to the innumerable grains on a beach. The consequences, sometimes, are terrifying.

Under the beneficent influence of the Company, our customs have become thoroughly impregnated with chance. The buyer of a dozen amphoras of Damascus wine will not be surprised if one of them contains a talisman or a viper. The scribe who draws up a contract scarcely ever fails to introduce some erroneous datum; I myself, in making this hasty declaration, have falsified or invented some grandeur, some atrocity; perhaps, too, a certain mysterious monotony. ...

Our historians, the most discerning in the world, have invented a method for correcting chance. It is well known that the operations of this method are (in general) trustworthy; although, naturally, they are not divulged without a measure of deceit. In any case, there is nothing so contaminated with fiction as the history of the Company. ...

A paleographic document, unearthed in a temple, may well be the work of yesterday's drawing or that of one lasting a century. No book is ever published without some variant in each copy. Scribes take a secret oath to omit, interpolate, vary.

The Company, with divine modesty, eludes all publicity. Its agents, as is only natural, are secret. The orders which it is continually sending out do not differ from those lavishly issued by imposters. Besides, who can ever boast of being a mere imposter? The inebriate who improvises an absurd mandate, the dreamer who suddenly awakes to choke the woman who lies at his side to death, do they not both, perhaps, carry out a secret decision by the Company? This silent functioning, comparable to that of God, gives rise to all manner of conjectures. One of them, for instance, abominably insinuates that the Company is eternal and that it will last until the last night of the world, when the last god annihilates the cosmos. Still another conjecture declares that the Company is omnipotent, but that it exerts its influence only in the most minute matters: in a bird's cry, in the shades of rust and the hues of dust, in the cat naps of dawn. There is one conjecture, spoken from the mouths of masked heresiarchs, to the effect that *the Company has never existed and never will*. A conjecture no less vile argues that it is indifferently inconsequential to affirm or deny the reality of the shadowy corporation, because Babylon is nothing but an infinite game of chance.

Translated by ANTHONY KERRIGAN

AN EXAMINATION OF THE WORK OF HERBERT QUAIN

Herbert Quain has just died at Roscommon. I was not astonished to find that the *Times Literary Supplement* allots him scarcely half a column of necrological piety, and that not a single laudatory epithet but is corrected (or seriously qualified) by an adverb. *The Spectator*, in its pertinent issue, is unquestionably less laconic and perhaps even more cordial, but it compares Quain's first book, *The God of the Labyrinth*, with a work by Mrs Agatha Christie, and others with books by Gertrude Stein: evocations which no one would consider inevitable and which would not have gratified the deceased. Quain, for that matter, was not a man who ever considered himself a genius; not even on those extravagant nights of literary conversation on which a man who has already worn out the printing presses inevitably plays at being Monsieur Teste or Doctor Sam Johnson. . . . He was very clear-headed about the experimental nature of his books: he thought them admirable, perhaps, for their novelty and for a certain laconic probity, but not for their passion.

'I am like Cowley's *Odes*,' he wrote me from Longford on 6 March, 1939. 'I do not belong to Art, but merely to the history of art.' In his mind, there was no discipline inferior to history.

I have transcribed one of Herbert Quain's modest statements. Naturally, this bit of modesty is not exhaustive of his thought. Flaubert and Henry James have accustomed us to suppose that works of art are infrequent and laboriously composed. The sixteenth century (we need only recall Cervantes' *Viaje al Parnaso*, or Shakespeare's destiny) did not share this disconsolate opinion. Neither did Herbert Quain. He thought that good literature was common enough, that there is scarce a dialogue in the street which does not achieve it. He also thought that the aesthetic act cannot be carried out without some element of astonishment, and that to be astonished by rote is difficult. With smiling earnestness he deplored 'the servile and obstinate conservation' of books from the past. ... I do not know if his vague theory is justifiable. I *do* know that his books are over-anxious to astonish.

I deeply lament having lent, irretrievably, the first book he published, to a female acquaintance. I have already said that it was a detective story. I may add that *The God of the Labyrinth* was issued by the publisher in the last days of November, 1933. During the first days of December of the same year, London and New York were enthralled by the agreeable and arduous involutions of *The Siamese Twin Mystery*. I prefer to attribute the failure of our friend's novel to this ruinous coincidence. Also (I wish to be entirely sincere) I would mention the deficient execution and the vain and frigid pomp of certain descriptions of the sea. At the end of seven years, it is impossible for me to recuperate the details of the action. But I will outline its plot, exactly as my forgetfulness now impoverishes (exactly as it now purifies) it. An indecipherable assassination takes place in the initial pages; a leisurely discussion takes place towards the middle; a solution appears in the end. Once the enigma is cleared up, there is a long and retrospective paragraph which contains the following phrase:

'Everyone thought that the encounter of the two chess players was accidental.' This phrase allows one to understand that the solution is erroneous. The unquiet reader re-reads the pertinent chapters and discovers *another* solution, the true one. The reader of this singular book is thus forcibly more discerning than the detective.

Even more heterodox is the 'regressive, ramified novel' titled *April March*, whose third (and only) part is dated 1936. In judging this novel, no one would fail to discover that it is a game; it is only fair to remember that the author never considered it anything else.

'I lay claim in this novel,' I have heard him say, 'to the essential features of all games: symmetry, arbitrary rules, tedium.' Even the title of the book is a feeble pun: it does not mean *the march of April*, but literally March–April. Someone has perceived an echo of Dunne's doctrines; Quain's prologue prefers to evoke the inverse world of Bradley in which death

precedes birth, the scar the wound, and the wound the blow
(*Appearance and Reality*, 1897, page 215).* The worlds
proposed by *April March* are not regressive; only the manner of
writing their history is so: regressive and ramified, as I have
already said. The work is made up of thirteen chapters. The
first reports the ambiguous dialogue of certain strangers on a
railway platform. The second narrates the events on the eve of
the first act. The third, also retrogade, describes the events of
another possible eve to the first day; the fourth, still another.
Each one of these three eves (each of which rigorously excludes
the other) is divided into three other eves, each of a very
different kind. The entire work, thus, constitutes nine novels;
each novel contains three long chapters. (The first chapter,
naturally, is common to all.) The temper of one of these novels
is symbolic; that of another, psychological; of another, communist; of still another, anti-communist; and so on. Perhaps a
diagram will help towards comprehending the structure:

$$
z \begin{cases} y\,1 & \begin{cases} x\,1 \\ x\,2 \\ x\,3 \end{cases} \\ \\ y\,2 & \begin{cases} x\,4 \\ x\,5 \\ x\,6 \end{cases} \\ \\ y\,3 & \begin{cases} x\,7 \\ x\,8 \\ x\,9 \end{cases} \end{cases}
$$

* Woe to Herbert Quain's erudition; woe to page 215 in a book dated 1897!
An interlocutor of Plato's Politician had already described a similar
regression: that of the Sons of the Earth or Autochthons, who, subjected to
the influence of an inverse rotation of the cosmos, passed from old age to
maturity, from maturity to childhood, from childhood to disappearance and
nothingness. Theopompus, too, in his *Philippics*, speaks of certain boreal
fruits which originate in those who eat them: the same retrogade process. . . .
It is even more interesting to imagine an inversion of Time: a state in which
we remember the future, and know nothing, or barely feel a presentiment, of
the past. Cf. the Tenth Canto of the *Inferno*, verses 97–102, where prophetic
vision is compared to presbyopia.

Concerning this structure we might well repeat what Schopenhauer declared of the twelve Kantian categories: everything is sacrificed to a rage for symmetry. Quite naturally, some of the nine stories are unworthy of Quain. The best piece is not the one he originally planned, $x\,4$; but rather one of a fantastic nature, $x\,9$. Certain others are deformed by slow-witted and languid jests or by useless pseudo-exactitudes. Whoever reads the sections in chronological order (for instance: $x\,3, y\,1, z$) will lose the peculiar savour of this strange book. Two narratives – $x\,7, x\,8$ – lack individual worth; mere juxtaposition lends them effectiveness. ...

I do not know if I should mention that once *April March* was published, Quain regretted the ternary order and predicted that whoever would imitate him would choose a binary arrangement:

$$z \begin{cases} y\,1 & \begin{cases} x\,1 \\ x\,2 \end{cases} \\[2em] y\,2 & \begin{cases} x\,3 \\ x\,4 \end{cases} \end{cases}$$

And that demiurges and gods would choose an infinite scheme: infinite stories, infinitely divided.

Highly diverse, but also retrospective, is the heroic comedy in two acts, *The Secret Mirror*. In the works already reviewed, the formal complexity had hindered the author's imagination; in this book, his evolution is freer. The first act (the most extensive) takes place at the country estate belonging to General Thrale, C.I.E., near Melton Mowbray. The invisible centre of the plot is Miss Ulrica Thrale, eldest daughter of the general. She is depicted for us, through certain lines of dialogue, as an arrogant horsewoman; we suspect that she does not cultivate literature; the newspapers announce her engagement to the Duke of Rutland; the same newspapers deny the engagement. She is revered by a playwright, Wilfred Quarles; she has favoured him, once or twice, with a distracted kiss. The characters possess vast fortunes and ancient blood;

their emotions are noble, though vehement; the dialogue seems to vacillate between the mere verbosity of Bulwer-Lytton and the epigrams of Wilde or Mr Philip Guedalla. There are a nightingale and a night; there is also a secret duel on a terrace. (Almost totally imperceptible, some curious contradiction exists, as do certain sordid details.) The characters of the first act appear in the second – bearing other names. The 'dramatic author' Wilfred Quarles is a commission agent in Liverpool; his real name is John William Quigley. Miss Thrale really does exist; Quigley has never seen her, but he morbidly collects photographs of her from *The Tatler* or *The Sketch*. Quigley is author of the first act. The unlikely or improbable 'country estate' is the Irish–Jewish boarding-house, transfigured and magnified by him, in which he lives. . . .

The texture of the acts is parallel, but in the second everything becomes slightly horrible, everything is postponed or frustrated. When *The Secret Mirror* opened, the critics pronounced the names of Freud and Julien Green. The mention of the first strikes me as totally unjustified.

Rumour had it that *The Secret Mirror* was a Freudian comedy; this propitious (and fallacious) interpretation determined its success. Unfortunately, Quain had already reached the age of forty; he was totally used to failure and he did not easily resign himself to a change of regime. He resolved to avenge himself. Towards the end of 1939 he issued *Statements*: perhaps the most original of his works, doubtless the least praised and most secret. Quain was in the habit of arguing that readers were an already extinct species.

'Every European,' he reasoned, 'is a writer, potentially or in fact.' He also affirmed that of the various pleasures offered by literature, the greatest is invention. Since not everyone is capable of this pleasure, many must content themselves with shams. For these 'imperfect writers', whose name is legion, Quain wrote the eight stories in *Statements*. Each of them prefigures or promises a good plot, deliberately frustrated by the author. One of them – not the best – insinuates *two* arguments. The reader, led astray by vanity, thinks he has invented them. I was ingenious enough to extract from the third, 'The Rose of Yesterday', my story of 'The Circular Ruins'.

1941   *Translated by* ANTHONY KERRIGAN

THE LIBRARY OF BABEL*

By this art you may contemplate
the variation of the 23 letters . . .
The Anatomy of Melancholy,
Part 2, Sect. II, Mem. IV.

The universe (which others call the Library) is composed of an indefinite, perhaps an infinite, number of hexagonal galleries, with enormous ventilation shafts in the middle, encircled by very low railings. From any hexagon the upper or lower stories are visible, interminably. The distribution of the galleries is invariable. Twenty shelves – five long shelves per side – cover all sides except two; their height, which is that of each floor, scarcely exceeds that of an average librarian. One of the free sides gives upon a narrow entrance way, which leads to another gallery, identical to the first and to all the others. To the left and to the right of the entrance way are two miniature rooms. One allows standing room for sleeping; the other, the satisfaction of fecal necessities. Through this section passes the spiral staircase, which plunges down into the abyss and rises up to the heights. In the entrance way hangs a mirror, which faithfully duplicates appearances. People are in the habit of inferring from this mirror that the Library is not infinite (if it really were, why this illusory duplication?); I prefer to dream that the polished surfaces feign and promise infinity. . . .

Light comes from some spherical fruits called by the name of lamps. There are two, running transversally, in each hexagon. The light they emit is insufficient, incessant.

Like all men of the Library, I have travelled in my youth. I have journeyed in search of a book, perhaps of the catalogue of catalogues; now that my eyes can scarcely decipher what I write, I am preparing to die a few leagues from the hexagon in

* It should, perhaps, be recalled that for years Jorge Luis Borges has been director of the National Library of Argentina. – *Editor's note.*

which I was born. Once dead, there will not lack pious hands to hurl me over the banister; my sepulchre shall be the unfathomable air: my body will sink lengthily and will corrupt and dissolve in the wind engendered by the fall, which is infinite. I affirm that the Library is interminable. The idealists argue that the hexagonal halls are a necessary form of absolute space or, at least, of our intuition of space. They contend that a triangular or pentagonal hall is inconceivable. (The mystics claim that to them ecstasy reveals a round chamber containing a great book with a continuous back circling the walls of the room; but their testimony is suspect; their words, obscure. That cyclical book is God.) Let it suffice me, for the time being, to repeat the classic dictum: *The Library is a sphere whose consummate centre is any hexagon, and whose circumference is inaccessible.*

Five shelves correspond to each one of the walls of each hexagon; each shelf contains thirty-two books of a uniform format; each book is made up of four hundred and ten pages; each page, of forty lines; each line, of some eighty black letters. There are also letters on the spine of each book; these letters do not indicate or prefigure what the pages will say. I know that such a lack of relevance, at one time, seemed mysterious. Before summarizing the solution (whose disclosure, despite its tragic implications, is perhaps the capital fact of this history), I want to recall certain axioms.

The first: The Library exists *ab aeterno.* No reasonable mind can doubt this truth, whose immediate corollary is the future eternity of the world. Man, the imperfect librarian, may be the work of chance or of malevolent demiurges; the universe, with its elegant endowment of shelves, of enigmatic volumes, of indefatigable ladders for the voyager, and of privies for the seated librarian, can only be the work of a god. In order to perceive the distance which exists between the divine and the human, it is enough to compare the rude tremulous symbols which my fallible hand scribbles on the end pages of a book with the organic letters inside: exact, delicate, intensely black, inimitably symmetric.

The second: *The number of orthographic symbols is twenty-*

five.* This bit of evidence permitted the formulation, three hundred years ago, of a general theory of the Library and the satisfactory resolution of the problem which no conjecture had yet made clear: the formless and chaotic nature of almost all books. One of these books, which my father saw in a hexagon of the circuit number fifteen ninety-four, was composed of the letters MCV perversely repeated from the first line to the last. Another, very much consulted in this zone, is a mere labyrinth of letters, but on the next-to-the-last page, one may read *O Time your pyramids*. As is well-known: for one reasonable line or one straightforward note there are leagues of insensate cacophony, of verbal farragoes and incoherencies. (I know of a wild region whose librarians repudiate the vain superstitious custom of seeking any sense in books and compare it to looking for meaning in dreams or in the chaotic lines of one's hands. ... They admit that the inventors of writing imitated the twenty-five natural symbols, but they maintain that this application is accidental and that books in themselves mean nothing. This opinion – we shall see – is not altogether false.)

For a long time it was believed that these impenetrable books belonged to past or remote languages. It is true that the most ancient men, the first librarians, made use of a language quite different from the one we speak today; it is true that some miles to the right the language is dialectical and that ninety stories up it is incomprehensible. All this, I repeat, is true; but four hundred and ten pages of unvarying MCVs do not correspond to any language, however dialectical or rudimentary it might be. Some librarians insinuated that each letter could influence the next, and that the value of MCV on the third line of page 71 was not the same as that of the same series in another position on another page; but this vague thesis did not prosper. Still other men thought in terms of

* The original manuscript of the present note does not contain digits or capital letters. The punctuation is limited to the comma and the period. These two signs, plus the space sign, and the twenty-two letters of the alphabet, make up the twenty-five sufficient symbols enumerated by the unknown author.

cryptographs; this conjecture has come to be universally accepted, though not in the sense in which it was formulated by its inventors.

Five hundred years ago, the chief of an upper hexagon* came upon a book as confusing as all the rest but which contained nearly two pages of homogeneous lines. He showed his find to an ambulant decipherer, who told him the lines were written in Portuguese. Others told him they were in Yiddish. In less than a century the nature of the language was finally established: it was a Samoyed-Lithuanian dialect of Guaraní, with classical Arabic inflections. The contents were also deciphered: notions of combinational analysis, illustrated by examples of variations with unlimited repetition. These examples made it possible for a librarian of genius to discover the fundamental law of the Library. This thinker observed that all the books, however diverse, are made up of uniform elements: the period, the comma, the space, the twenty-two letters of the alphabet. He also adduced a circumstance confirmed by all travellers: *There are not, in the whole vast Library, two identical books.* From all these incontrovertible premises he deduced that the Library is total and that its shelves contain all the possible combinations of the twenty-odd orthographic symbols (whose number, though vast, is not infinite); that is, everything which can be expressed, in all languages. Everything is there: the minute history of the future, the autobiographies of the archangels, the faithful catalogue of the Library, thousands and thousands of false catalogues, a demonstration of the fallacy of these catalogues, a demonstration of the fallacy of the true catalogue, the Gnostic gospel of Basilides, the commentary on this gospel, the commentary on the commentary of this gospel, the veridical account of your death, a version of each book in all languages, the interpolations of every book in all books.

* Formerly, for each three hexagons there was one man. Suicide and pulmonary diseases have destroyed this proportion. My memory recalls scenes of unspeakable melancholy: there have been many nights when I have ventured down corridors and polished staircases without encountering a single librarian.

When it was proclaimed that the Library comprised all books, the first impression was one of extravagant joy. All men felt themselves lords of a secret, intact treasure. There was no personal or universal problem whose eloquent solution did not exist – in some hexagon. The universe was justified, the universe suddenly expanded to the limitless dimensions of hope. At that time there was much talk of the Vindications: books of apology and prophecy, which vindicated for all time the actions of every man in the world and established a store of prodigious arcana for the future. Thousands of covetous persons abandoned their dear natal hexagons and crowded up the stairs, urged on by the vain aim of finding their Vindication. These pilgrims disputed in the narrow corridors, hurled dark maledictions, strangled each other on the divine stairways, flung the deceitful books to the bottom of the tunnels, and died as they were thrown into space by men from remote regions. Some went mad. . . .

The Vindications do exist. I have myself seen two of these books, which were concerned with future people, people who were perhaps not imaginary. But the searchers did not remember that the calculable possibility of a man's finding his own book, or some perfidious variation of his own book, is close to zero.

The clarification of the basic mysteries of humanity – the origin of the Library and of time – was also expected. It is credible that those grave mysteries can be explained in words: if the language of the philosophers does not suffice, the multiform Library will have produced the unexpected language required and the necessary vocabularies and grammars for this language.

It is now four centuries since men have been wearying the hexagons. . . .

There are official searchers, *inquisitors*. I have observed them carrying out their functions: they are always exhausted. They speak of a staircase without steps where they were almost killed. They speak of galleries and stairs with the local librarian. From time to time they will pick up the nearest book and leaf through its pages, in search of infamous words. Obviously, no one expects to discover anything.

The uncommon hope was followed, naturally enough, by deep depression. The certainty that some shelf in some hexagon contained precious books and that these books were inaccessible seemed almost intolerable. A blasphemous sect suggested that all searches be given up and that men everywhere shuffle letters and symbols until they succeeded in composing, by means of an improbable stroke of luck, the canonical books. The authorities found themselves obliged to issue severe orders. The sect disappeared, but in my childhood I still saw old men who would hide out in the privies for long periods of time, and, with metal discs in a forbidden dicebox, feebly mimic the divine disorder.

Other men, inversely, thought that the primary task was to eliminate useless works. They would invade the hexagons, exhibiting credentials which were not always false, skim through a volume with annoyance, and then condemn entire bookshelves to destruction: their ascetic, hygienic fury is responsible for the senseless loss of millions of books. Their name is execrated; but those who mourn the 'treasures' destroyed by this frenzy overlook two notorious facts. One: the Library is so enormous that any reduction undertaken by humans is infinitesimal. Two: each book is unique, irreplaceable, but (inasmuch as the Library is total) there are always several hundreds of thousands of imperfect facsimiles – of works which differ only by one letter or one comma. Contrary to public opinion, I dare suppose that the consequences of the depredations committed by the Purifiers have been exaggerated by the horror which these fanatics provoked. They were spurred by the delirium of storming the books in the Crimson Hexagon: books of a smaller than ordinary format, omnipotent, illustrated, magical.

We know, too, of another superstition of that time: the Man of the Book. In some shelf of some hexagon, men reasoned, there must exist a book which is the cipher and perfect compendium of *all the rest*: some librarian has perused it, and it is analogous to a god. Vestiges of the worship of that

remote functionary still persist in the language of this zone.
Many pilgrimages have sought Him out. For a century they
trod the most diverse routes in vain. How to locate the secret
hexagon which harboured it? Someone proposed a regressive
approach: in order to locate book A, first consult book B
which will indicate the location of A; in order to locate book
B, first consult book C, and so on ad infinitum. ...

I have squandered and consumed my years in adventures
of this type. To me, it does not seem unlikely that on some
shelf of the universe there lies a total book.* I pray the
unknown gods that some man – even if only one man, and
though it may have been thousands of years ago! – may have
examined and read it. If honour and wisdom and happiness
are not for me, let them be for others. May heaven exist,
though my place be in hell. Let me be outraged and
annihilated, but may Thy enormous Library be justified, for
one instant, in one being.

The impious assert that absurdities are the norm in the
Library and that anything reasonable (even humble and pure
coherence) is an almost miraculous exception. They speak (I
know) of 'the febrile Library, whose hazardous volumes run
the constant risk of being changed into others and in which
everything is affirmed, denied, and confused as by a divinity
in delirium.' These words, which not only denounce disorder
but exemplify it as well, manifestly demonstrate the bad taste
of the speakers and their desperate ignorance. Actually, the
Library includes all verbal structures, all the variations
allowed by the twenty-five orthographic symbols, but it does
not permit of one absolute absurdity. It is pointless to observe
that the best book in the numerous hexagons under my
administration is entitled *Combed Clap of Thunder*; or that
another is called *The Plaster Cramp*; and still another *Axaxaxas
Mlö*. Such propositions as are contained in these titles, at first
sight incoherent, doubtless yield a cryptographic or allegori-

* I repeat: it is enough that a book be possible for it to exist. Only the
impossible is excluded. For example: no book is also a stairway, though
doubtless there are books that discuss and deny and demonstrate this
possibility and others whose structure corresponds to that of a stairway.

cal justification. Since they are verbal, these justifications already figure, *ex hypothesi*, in the Library. I cannot combine certain letters, as *dhcmrlchtdj*, which the divine Library has not already foreseen in combination, and which in one of its secret languages does not encompass some terrible meaning. No one can articulate a syllable which is not full of tenderness and fear, and which is not, in one of those languages, the powerful name of some god. To speak is to fall into tautologies. This useless and wordy epistle itself already exists in one of the thirty volumes of the five shelves in one of the uncountable hexagons – and so does its refutation. (And *n* number of possible languages make use of the same vocabulary; in some of them, the symbol *library* admits of the correct definition *ubiquitous and everlasting system of hexagonal galleries*, but *library* is *bread* or *pyramid* or anything else, and the seven words which define it possess another value. You who read me, are you sure you understand my language?)

Methodical writing distracts me from the present condition of men. But the certainty that everything has been already written nullifies or makes phantoms of us all. I know of districts where the youth prostrate themselves before books and barbarously kiss the pages, though they do not know how to make out a single letter. Epidemics, heretical disagreements, the pilgrimages which inevitably degenerate into banditry, have decimated the population. I believe I have mentioned the suicides, more frequent each year. Perhaps I am deceived by old age and fear, but I suspect that the human species – the unique human species – is on the road to extinction, while the Library will last on forever: illuminated, solitary, infinite, perfectly immovable, filled with precious volumes, useless, incorruptible, secret.

Infinite I have just written. I have not interpolated this adjective merely from rhetorical habit. It is not illogical, I say, to think that the world is infinite. Those who judge it to be limited postulate that in remote places the corridors and stairs and hexagons could inconceivably cease – a manifest absurdity. Those who imagined it to be limitless forget that the possible number of books is limited. I dare insinuate the following solution to this ancient problem: *The Library is limitless and periodic*. If an eternal voyager were to traverse it in any direction, he would find, after many centuries, that the same volumes are repeated in the same disorder (which, repeated, would constitute an order: Order itself). My solitude rejoices in this elegant hope.*

Mar del Plata
1941   *Translated by* ANTHONY KERRIGAN

* Letizia Alvarez de Toledo has observed that the vast Library is useless. Strictly speaking, *one single volume* should suffice: a single volume of ordinary format, printed in nine or ten type body, and consisting of an infinite number of infinitely thin pages. (At the beginning of the seventeenth century, Cavalieri said that any solid body is the superposition of an infinite number of planes.) This silky vade mecum would scarcely be handy: each apparent leaf of the book would divide into other analogous leaves. The inconceivable central leaf would have no reverse.

THE GARDEN OF FORKING PATHS

To Victoria Ocampo

In his *A History of the World War* (page 22), Captain Liddell Hart reports that a planned offensive by thirteen British divisions, supported by fourteen hundred artillery pieces, against the German line at Serre-Montauban, scheduled for July 24, 1916, had to be postponed until the morning of the 29th. He comments that torrential rain caused this delay – which lacked any special significance. The following deposition, dictated by, read over, and then signed by Dr Yu Tsun, former teacher of English at the Tsingtao *Hochschule*, casts unsuspected light upon this event. The first two pages are missing.

*

. . . and I hung up the phone. Immediately I recollected the voice that had spoken in German. It was that of Captain Richard Madden. Madden, in Viktor Runeberg's office, meant the end of all our work and – though this seemed a secondary matter, *or should have seemed so to me* – of our lives also. His being there meant that Runeberg had been arrested or murdered.* Before the sun set on this same day, I ran the same risk. Madden was implacable. Rather, to be more accurate, he was obliged to be implacable. An Irishman in the service of England, a man suspected of equivocal feelings if not of actual treachery, how could he fail to welcome and seize upon this extraordinary piece of luck: the discovery, capture and perhaps the deaths of two agents of Imperial Germany?

I went up to my bedroom. Absurd though the gesture was, I closed and locked the door. I threw myself down on my narrow iron bed, and waited on my back. The never changing

---

* A malicious and outlandish statement. In point of fact, Captain Richard Madden had been attacked by the Prussian spy Hans Rabener, alias Viktor Runeberg, who drew an automatic pistol when Madden appeared with orders for the spy's arrest. Madden, in self defence, had inflicted wounds of which the spy later died. – *Note by the manuscript editor.*

rooftops filled the window, and the hazy six o'clock sun hung in the sky. It seemed incredible that this day, a day without warnings or omens, might be that of my implacable death. In despite of my dead father, in despite of having been a child in one of the symmetrical gardens of Hai Feng, was I to die now?

Then I reflected that all things happen, happen to one, precisely *now*. Century follows century, and things happen only in the present. There are countless men in the air, on land and at sea, and all that really happens happens to me. . . . The almost unbearable memory of Madden's long horse-face put an end to these wandering thoughts.

In the midst of my hatred and terror (now that it no longer matters to me to speak of terror, now that I have outwitted Richard Madden, now that my neck hankers for the hangman's noose), I knew that the fast-moving and doubtless happy soldier did not suspect that I possessed the Secret – the name of the exact site of the new British artillery park on the Ancre. A bird streaked across the misty sky and, absently, I turned it into an airplane and then that airplane into many in the skies of France, shattering the artillery park under a rain of bombs. If only my mouth, before it should be silenced by a bullet, could shout this name in such a way that it could be heard in Germany. . . . My voice, my human voice, was weak. How could it reach the ear of the Chief? The ear of that sick and hateful man who knew nothing of Runeberg or of me except that we were in Staffordshire. A man who, sitting in his arid Berlin office, leafed infinitely through newspapers, looking in vain for news from us. I said aloud, 'I must flee.'

I sat up on the bed, in senseless and perfect silence, as if Madden was already peering at me. Something – perhaps merely a desire to prove my total penury to myself – made me empty out my pockets. I found just what I knew I was going to find. The American watch, the nickel-plated chain and the square coin, the key ring with the useless but compromising keys to Runeberg's office, the notebook, a letter which I decided to destroy at once (and which I did not destroy), a five shilling piece, two single shillings and some pennies, a red and blue pencil, a handkerchief – and a revolver with a single bullet. Absurdly I held it and weighed it in my hand, to give myself courage. Vaguely I thought that a pistol shot can be heard for a great distance.

In ten minutes I had developed my plan. The telephone directory gave me the name of the one person capable of passing on the information. He lived in a suburb of Fenton, less than half an hour away by train.

I am a timorous man. I can say it now, now that I have brought my incredibly risky plan to an end. It was not easy to bring about, and I know that its execution was terrible. I did not do it for Germany – no! Such a barbarous country is of no importance to me, particularly since it had degraded me by making me become a spy. Furthermore, I knew an Englishman – a modest man – who, for me, is as great as Goethe. I did not speak with him for more than an hour, but during that time, he *was* Goethe.

I carried out my plan because I felt the Chief had some fear of those of my race, of those uncountable forebears whose culmination lies in me. I wished to prove to him that a yellow man could save his armies. Besides, I had to escape the Captain. His hands and voice could, at any moment, knock and beckon at my door.

Silently, I dressed, took leave of myself in the mirror, went down the stairs, sneaked a look at the quiet street, and went out. The station was not far from my house, but I thought it more prudent to take a cab. I told myself that I thus ran less chance of being recognized. The truth is that, in the deserted street, I felt infinitely visible and vulnerable. I recall that I told the driver to stop short of the main entrance. I got out with a painful and deliberate slowness.

I was going to the village of Ashgrove, but took a ticket for a station further on. The train would leave in a few minutes, at eight-fifty. I hurried, for the next would not go until half past nine. There was almost no one on the platform. I walked through the carriages. I remember some farmers, a woman dressed in mourning, a youth deep in Tacitus' *Annals* and a wounded, happy soldier.

At last the train pulled out. A man I recognized ran

furiously, but vainly, the length of the platform. It was
Captain Richard Madden. Shattered, trembling, I huddled in
the distant corner of the seat, as far as possible from the
fearful window.

From utter terror I passed into a state of almost abject
happiness. I told myself that the duel had already started and
that I had won the first encounter by besting my adversary in
his first attack – even if it was for only forty minutes – by an
accident of fate. I argued that so small a victory prefigured a
total victory. I argued that it was not so trivial, that were it not
for the precious accident of the train schedule, I would be in
prison or dead. I argued, with no less sophism, that my
timorous happiness was proof that I was man enough to bring
this adventure to a successful conclusion. From my weakness
I drew strength that never left me.

I foresee that man will resign himself each day to new
abominations, that soon only soldiers and bandits will be left.
To them I offer this advice: *Whosoever would undertake some
atrocious enterprise should act as if it were already accomplished,
should impose upon himself a future as irrevocable as the past.*

Thus I proceeded, while with the eyes of a man already
dead, I contemplated the fluctuations of the day which would
probably be my last, and watched the diffuse coming of night.

The train crept along gently, amid ash trees. It slowed
down and stopped, almost in the middle of a field. No one
called the name of a station. 'Ashgrove?' I asked some
children on the platform. 'Ashgrove,' they replied. I got out.

A lamp lit the platform, but the children's faces remained
in a shadow. One of them asked me: 'Are you going to Dr
Stephen Albert's house?' Without waiting for my answer,
another said: 'The house is a good distance away but you
won't get lost if you take the road to the left and bear to the
left at every crossroad.' I threw them a coin (my last), went
down some stone steps and started along a deserted road. At a
slight incline, the road ran downhill. It was a plain dirt way,
and overhead the branches of trees intermingled, while a
round moon hung low in the sky as if to keep me company.

For a moment I thought that Richard Madden might in

some way have divined my desperate intent. At once I realized that this would be impossible. The advice about turning always to the left reminded me that such was the common formula for finding the central courtyard of certain labyrinths. I know something about labyrinths. Not for nothing am I the great-grandson of Ts'ui Pên. He was Governor of Yunnan and gave up temporal power to write a novel with more characters than there are in the *Hung Lou Mêng*, and to create a maze in which all men would lose themselves. He spent thirteen years on these oddly assorted tasks before he was assassinated by a stranger. His novel had no sense to it and nobody ever found his labyrinth.

Under the trees of England I meditated on this lost and perhaps mythical labyrinth. I imagined it untouched and perfect on the secret summit of some mountain; I imagined it drowned under rice paddies or beneath the sea; I imagined it infinite, made not only of eight-sided pavilions and of twisting paths but also of rivers, provinces and kingdoms. ... I thought of a maze of mazes, of a sinuous, ever growing maze which would take in both past and future and would somehow involve the stars.

Lost in these imaginary illusions I forgot my destiny – that of the hunted. For an undetermined period of time I felt myself cut off from the world, an abstract spectator. The hazy and murmuring countryside, the moon, the decline of the evening, stirred within me. Going down the gently sloping road I could not feel fatigue. The evening was at once intimate and infinite.

The road kept descending and branching off, through meadows misty in the twilight. A high-pitched and almost syllabic music kept coming and going, moving with the breeze, blurred by the leaves and by distance.

I thought that a man might be an enemy of other men, of the differing moments of other men, but never an enemy of a country: not of fireflies, words, gardens, streams, or the West wind.

Meditating thus I arrived at a high, rusty iron gate. Through the railings I could see an avenue bordered with poplar trees and also a kind of summer house or pavilion. Two things dawned on me at once, the first trivial and the second almost incredible: the music came from the pavilion and that music was Chinese. That was why I had accepted it fully, without paying it any attention. I do not remember whether there was a bell, a push-button, or whether I attracted attention by clapping my hands. The stuttering sparks of the music kept on.

But from the end of the avenue, from the main house a lantern approached; a lantern which alternately, from moment to moment, was crisscrossed or put out by the trunks of the trees; a paper lantern shaped like a drum and coloured like the moon. A tall man carried it. I could not see his face, for the light blinded me.

He opened the gate and spoke slowly in my language.

'I see that the worthy Hsi P'eng has troubled himself to see to relieving my solitude. No doubt you want to see the garden?'

Recognizing the name of one of our consuls, I replied, somewhat taken aback.

'The garden?'

'The garden of forking paths.'

Something stirred in my memory and I said, with incomprehensible assurance:

'The garden of my ancestor, Ts'ui Pên.'

'Your ancestor? Your illustrious ancestor? Come in.'

The damp path zigzagged like those of my childhood. When we reached the house, we went into a library filled with books from both East and West. I recognized some large volumes bound in yellow silk – manuscripts of the Lost Encyclopedia which was edited by the Third Emperor of the Luminous Dynasty. They had never been printed. A phonograph record was spinning near a bronze phoenix. I remember also a rose-glazed jar and yet another, older by many centuries, of that blue colour which our potters copied from the Persians. . . .

Stephen Albert was watching me with a smile on his face. He was, as I have said, remarkably tall. His face was deeply lined and he had grey eyes and a grey beard. There was about him something of the priest, and something of the sailor. Later, he told me he had been a missionary in Tientsin before he 'had aspired to become a Sinologist.'

We sat down, I upon a large, low divan, he with his back to the window and to a large circular clock. I calculated that my pursuer, Richard Madden, could not arrive in less than an hour. My irrevocable decision could wait.

'A strange destiny,' said Stephen Albert, 'that of Ts'ui Pên – Governor of his native province, learned in astronomy, in astrology and tireless in the interpretation of the canonical books, a chess player, a famous poet and a calligrapher. Yet he abandoned all to make a book and a labyrinth. He gave up all the pleasures of oppression, justice, of a well-stocked bed, of banquets, and even of erudition, and shut himself up in the Pavilion of Limpid Solitude for thirteen years. At his death, his heirs found only a mess of manuscripts. The family, as you doubtless know, wished to consign them to the fire, but the executor of the estate – a Taoist or a Buddhist monk – insisted on their publication.'

'Those of the blood of Ts'ui Pên,' I replied, 'still curse the memory of that monk. Such a publication was madness. The book is a shapeless mass of contradictory rough drafts. I examined it once upon a time: the hero dies in the third chapter, while in the fourth he is alive. As for that other enterprise of Ts'ui Pên ... his Labyrinth. ...'

'Here is the Labyrinth,' Albert said, pointing to a tall, lacquered writing cabinet.

'An ivory labyrinth?' I exclaimed. 'A tiny labyrinth indeed ... !'

'A symbolic labyrinth,' he corrected me. 'An invisible labyrinth of time. I, a barbarous Englishman, have been given the key to this transparent mystery. After more than a hundred years most of the details are irrecoverable, lost beyond all recall, but it isn't hard to imagine what must have happened. At one time, Ts'u Pên must have said: "I am going into seclusion to write a book," and at another, "I am retiring to construct a maze." Everyone assumed these were separate activities. No one realized that the book and the labyrinth were one and the same. The Pavilion of Limpid Solitude was set in the middle of an intricate garden. This may have suggested the idea of a physical maze.

'Ts'ui Pên died. In all the vast lands which once belonged to your family, no one could find the labyrinth. The novel's confusion suggested that *it* was the labyrinth. Two circumstances showed me the direct solution to the problem. First, the curious legend that Ts'ui Pên had proposed to create an infinite maze, second, a fragment of a letter which I discovered.'

Albert rose. For a few moments he turned his back to me. He opened the top drawer in the high black and gilded writing cabinet. He returned holding in his hand a piece of paper which had once been crimson but which had faded with the passage of time: it was rose coloured, tenuous, quadrangular. Ts'ui Pên's calligraphy was justly famous. Eagerly, but without understanding, I read the words which a man of my blood had written with a small brush: 'I leave to various future times, but not to all, my garden of forking paths.'

I handed back the sheet of paper in silence. Albert went on:

'Before I discovered this letter, I kept asking myself how a book could be infinite. I could not imagine any other than a cyclic volume, circular. A volume whose last page would be the same as the first and so have the possibility of continuing indefinitely. I recalled, too, the night in the middle of *The Thousand and One Nights* when Queen Scheherazade, through a magical mistake on the part of her copyist, started to tell the story of *The Thousand and One Nights*, with the risk of again arriving at the night upon which she will relate it, and thus on to infinity. I also imagined a Platonic hereditary work, passed on from father to son, to which each individual would add a new chapter or correct, with pious care, the work of his elders.

'These conjectures gave me amusement, but none seemed to have the remotest application to the contradictory chapters of Ts'ui Pên. At this point, I was sent from Oxford the manuscript you have just seen.

'Naturally, my attention was caught by the sentence, "I leave to various future times, but not to all, my garden of forking paths." I had no sooner read this, than I understood. *The Garden of Forking Paths* was the chaotic novel itself. The phrase "to various future times, but not to all" suggested the image of bifurcating in time, not in space. Rereading the whole work confirmed this theory. In all fiction, when a man is faced with alternatives he chooses one at the expense of the others. In the almost unfathomable Ts'ui Pên, he chooses – simultaneously – all of them. He thus *creates* various futures, various times which start others that will in their turn branch out and bifurcate in other times. This is the cause of the contradictions in the novel.

'Fang, let us say, has a secret. A stranger knocks at his door. Fang makes up his mind to kill him. Naturally there are various possible outcomes. Fang can kill the intruder, the intruder can kill Fang, both can be saved, both can die and so on and so on. In Ts'ui Pên's work, all the possible solutions occur, each one being the point of departure for other bifurcations. Sometimes the pathways of this labyrinth converge. For example, you come to this house; but in other possible pasts you are my enemy; in others my friend.

'If you will put up with my atrocious pronunciation, I would like to read you a few pages of your ancestor's work.'

His countenance, in the bright circle of lamplight, was certainly that of an ancient, but it shone with something unyielding, even immortal.

With slow precision, he read two versions of the same epic chapter. In the first, an army marches into battle over a desolate mountain pass. The bleak and sombre aspect of the rocky landscape made the soldiers feel that life itself was of little value, and so they won the battle easily. In the second, the same army passes through a palace where a banquet is in progress. The splendour of the feast remained a memory throughout the glorious battle, and so victory followed.

With proper veneration I listened to these old tales, although perhaps with less admiration for them in themselves than for the fact that they had been thought out by one of my own blood, and that a man of a distant empire had given them back to me, in the last stage of a desperate adventure, on a Western island. I remember the final words, repeated at the end of each version like a secret command: 'Thus the heroes fought, with tranquil heart and bloody sword. They were resigned to killing and dying.'

At that moment I felt within me and around me something invisible and intangible pullulating. It was not the pullulation of two divergent, parallel, and finally converging armies, but an agitation more inaccessible, more intimate, prefigured by them in some way. Stephen Albert continued:

'I do not think that your illustrious ancestor toyed idly with variations. I do not find it believable that he would waste thirteen years labouring over a never ending experiment in rhetoric. In your country the novel is an inferior genre; in Ts'ui Pên's period, it was a despised one. Ts'ui Pên was a fine novelist but he was also a man of letters who, doubtless, considered himself more than a mere novelist. The testimony of his contemporaries attests to this, and certainly the known facts of his life confirm his leanings towards the metaphysical and the mystical. Philosophical conjectures take up the greater part of his novel. I know that of all problems, none disquieted him more, and none concerned him more, than the profound one of time. Now then, this is the *only* problem that does not figure in the pages of *The Garden*. He does not even use the word which means *time*. How can these voluntary omissions be explained?'

I proposed various solutions, all of them inadequate. We discussed them. Finally Stephen Albert said: 'In a guessing game to which the answer is chess, which word is the only one prohibited?' I thought for a moment and then replied:

'The word is *chess*.'

'Precisely,' said Albert. '*The Garden of Forking Paths* is an enormous guessing game, or parable, in which the subject is time. The rules of the game forbid the use of the word itself. To eliminate a word completely, to refer to it by means of inept phrases and obvious paraphrases, is perhaps the best way of drawing attention to it. This, then, is the tortuous method of approach preferred by the oblique Ts'ui Pên in every meandering of his interminable novel. I have gone over hundreds of manuscripts, I have corrected errors introduced by careless copyists, I have worked out the plan from this chaos, I have restored, or believe I have restored, the original. I have translated the whole work. I can state categorically that not once has the word *time* been used in the whole book.

'The explanation is obvious. *The Garden of Forking Paths* is a picture, incomplete yet not false, of the universe such as Ts'ui Pên conceived it to be. Differing from Newton and Schopenhauer, your ancestor did not think of time as absolute and uniform. He believed in an infinite series of times, in a dizzily growing, ever spreading network of diverging, converging and parallel times. This web of time – the strands of which approach one another, bifurcate, intersect or ignore each other through the centuries – embraces *every* possibility. We do not exist in most of them. In some you exist and not I, while in others I do, and you do not, and in yet others both of us exist. In this one, in which chance has favoured me, you have come to my gate. In another, you, crossing the garden, have found me dead. In yet another, I say these very same words, but am an error, a phantom.'

'In all of them,' I enunciated, with a tremor in my voice. 'I deeply appreciate and am grateful to you for the restoration of Ts'ui Pên's garden.'

'Not in *all*,' he murmured with a smile. 'Time is forever dividing itself towards innumerable futures and in one of them I am your enemy.'

Once again I sensed the pullulation of which I have already spoken. It seemed to me that the dew-damp garden surrounding the house was infinitely saturated with invisible people. All were Albert and myself, secretive, busy and multiform in other dimensions of time. I lifted my eyes and the short nightmare disappeared. In the black and yellow garden there was only a single man, but this man was as strong as a statue and this man was walking up the path and he was Captain Richard Madden.

'The future exists now,' I replied. 'But I am your friend. Can I take another look at the letter?'

Albert rose from his seat. He stood up tall as he opened the top drawer of the high writing cabinet. For a moment his back was again turned to me. I had the revolver ready. I fired with the utmost care: Albert fell without a murmur, at once. I swear that his death was instantaneous, as if he had been struck by lightning.

What remains is unreal and unimportant. Madden broke in and arrested me. I have been condemned to hang. Abominably, I have yet triumphed! The secret name of the city to be attacked got through to Berlin. Yesterday it was bombed. I read the news in the same English newspapers which were trying to solve the riddle of the murder of the learned Sinologist Stephen Albert by the unknown Yu Tsun. The Chief, however, had already solved this mystery. He knew that my problem was to shout, with my feeble voice, above the tumult of war, the name of the city called Albert, and I had no other course open to me than to kill someone of that name. He does not know, for no one can, of my infinite penitence and sickness of the heart.

Translated by HELEN TEMPLE *and* RUTHVEN TODD

PART TWO
ARTIFICES

(1944)

PROLOGUE

Though less torpidly executed, the pieces in this section are similar to those which form the first part of the book. Two of them allow, perhaps, separate mention: 'Death and the Compass' and 'Funes, the Memorious.' The second is a long metaphor of insomnia. The first, despite the German or Scandinavian names, occurs in a Buenos Aires of dreams: the twisted Rue de Toulon is the Paseo de Julio; Triste-le-Roy is the hotel where Herbert Ashe received, and probably did not read, the eleventh volume of an illusory encyclopedia. After composing this narrative, I have come to consider the soundness of amplifying the time and space in which it occurs: vengeance could be inherited; the periods of time might be computed in years, perhaps in centuries; the first letter of the Name might be spoken in Iceland; the second in Mexico; the third in Hindustan. Should I add that the Hasidim included saints and that the sacrifice of four lives in order to obtain the four letters imposed by the Name is a fantasy dictated by the form of my story?

Postscript. 1956. I have added three stories to the series: 'The South', 'The Sect of the Phoenix', 'The End'. Apart from one character − Recabarren − whose immobility and passivity serve as a contrasting background, nothing or almost nothing in the brief course of the last-named is an invention of mine; everything in it is implicit in a famous book, and I have merely been the first to reveal, or at least to declare it. In the allegory of the Phoenix I imposed upon myself the problem of hinting at an ordinary fact − the Secret − in an irresolute and gradual manner, which, in the end, would prove to be unequivocal; I do not know how fortunate I have been. Of 'The South', which is perhaps my best story, let it suffice for me to suggest that it can be read as a direct narrative of novelistic events, and also in another way.

The heterogeneous census of the authors whom I con-tinually reread is made up of Schopenhauer, De Quincey,

Stevenson, Mauthner, Shaw, Chesterton, Léon Bloy. I
believe I perceive the remote influence of the last-mentioned
in the Christological fantasy entitled 'Three Versions of
Judas.'

Buenos Aires
29 August, 1944   J.L.B.

FUNES, THE MEMORIOUS

I remember him (I scarcely have the right to use this ghostly verb; only one man on earth deserved the right, and he is dead), I remember him with a dark passionflower in his hand, looking at it as no one has ever looked at such a flower, though they might look from the twilight of day until the twilight of night, for a whole life long. I remember him, his face immobile and Indian-like, and singularly *remote*, behind his cigarette. I remember (I believe) the strong delicate fingers of the plainsman who can braid leather. I remember, near those hands, a vessel in which to make maté tea, bearing the arms of the Banda Oriental;* I remember, in the window of the house, a yellow rush mat, and beyond, a vague marshy landscape. I remember clearly his voice, the deliberate, resentful nasal voice of the old Eastern Shore man, without the Italianate syllables of today. I did not see him more than three times; the last time, in 1887. . . .

That all those who knew him should write something about him seems to me a very felicitous idea; my testimony may perhaps be the briefest and without doubt the poorest, and it will not be the least impartial. The deplorable fact of my being an Argentinian will hinder me from falling into a dithyramb – an obligatory form in the Uruguay, when the theme is an Uruguayan.

Littérateur, slicker, Buenos Airean: Funes did not use these insulting phrases, but I am sufficiently aware that for him I represented these unfortunate categories. Pedro Leandro Ipuche has written that Funes was a precursor of the superman, 'an untamed and vernacular Zarathustra'; I do not doubt it, but one must not forget, either, that he was a countryman from the town of Fray Bentos, with certain incurable limitations.

My first recollection of Funes is quite clear: I see him at dusk, sometime in March or February of the year '84. That

* The Eastern Shore (of the Uruguay River); now the Orient Republic of Uruguay. – *Editor's note.*

year, my father had taken me to spend the summer at Fray
Bentos. I was on my way back from the farm at San Francisco
with my cousin Bernardo Haedo. We came back singing, on
horseback; and this last fact was not the only reason for my
joy. After a sultry day, an enormous slate-grey storm had
obscured the sky. It was driven on by a wind from the south;
the trees were already tossing like madmen; and I had the
apprehension (the secret hope) that the elemental downpour
would catch us out in the open. We were running a kind of
race with the tempest. We rode into a narrow lane which
wound down between two enormously high brick footpaths.
It had grown black of a sudden; I now heard rapid almost
secret steps above; I raised my eyes and saw a boy running
along the narrow, cracked path as if he were running along a
narrow, broken wall. I remember the loose trousers, tight at
the bottom, the hemp sandals; I remember the cigarette in the
hard visage, standing out against the by now limitless darkness. Bernardo unexpectedly yelled to him: 'What's the time,
Ireneo?' Without looking up, without stopping, Ireneo replied: 'In ten minutes it will be eight o'clock, child Bernardo
Juan Francisco.' The voice was sharp, mocking.

I am so absentminded that the dialogue which I have just
cited would not have penetrated my attention if it had not
been repeated by my cousin, who was stimulated, I think, by
a certain local pride and by a desire to show himself
indifferent to the other's three-sided reply.

He told me that the boy above us in the pass was a certain
Ireneo Funes, renowned for a number of eccentricities, such
as that of having nothing to do with people and of always
knowing the time, like a watch. He added that Ireneo was the
son of María Clementina Funes, an ironing woman in the
town, and that his father, some people said, was an 'Englishman' named O'Connor, a doctor in the salting fields, though
some said the father was a horse-breaker, or scout, from the
province of El Salto. Ireneo lived with his mother, at the edge
of the country house of the Laurels.

In the years '85 and '86 we spent the summer in the city of
Montevideo. We returned to Fray Bentos in '87. As was

natural, I inquired after all my acquaintances, and finally, about 'the chronometer Funes'. I was told that he had been thrown by a wild horse at the San Francisco ranch, and that he had been hopelessly crippled. I remember the impression of uneasy magic which the news provoked in me: the only time I had seen him we were on horseback, coming from San Francisco, and he was in a high place; from the lips of my cousin Bernardo the affair sounded like a dream elaborated with elements out of the past. They told me that Ireneo did not move now from his cot, but remained with his eyes fixed on the backyard fig tree, or on a cobweb. At sunset he allowed himself to be brought to the window. He carried pride to the extreme of pretending that the blow which had befallen him was a good thing. ... Twice I saw him behind the iron grate which sternly delineated his eternal imprisonment: unmoving, once, his eyes closed; unmoving also, another time, absorbed in the contemplation of a sweet-smelling sprig of lavender cotton.

At the time I had begun, not without some ostentation, the methodical study of Latin. My valise contained the *De viris illustribus* of Lhomond, the *Thesaurus* of Quicherat, Caesar's *Commentaries*, and an odd-numbered volume of the *Historia Naturalis* of Pliny, which exceeded (and still exceeds) my modest talents as a Latinist. Everything is noised around in a small town; Ireneo, at his small farm on the outskirts, was not long in learning of the arrival of these anomalous books. He sent me a flowery, ceremonious letter, in which he recalled our encounter, unfortunately brief, 'on the seventh day of February of the year '84,' and alluded to the glorious services which Don Gregorio Haedo, my uncle, dead the same year, 'had rendered to the Two Fatherlands in the glorious campaign of Ituzaingó,' and he solicited the loan of any one of the volumes, to be accompanied by a dictionary 'for the better intelligence of the original text, for I do not know Latin as yet.' He promised to return them in good condition, almost immediately. The letter was perfect, very nicely constructed; the orthography was of the type sponsored by Andrés Bello: *i* for *y, j* for *g*. At first I naturally suspected a jest. My cousins assured me it was not so, that these were the ways of Ireneo. I did not know whether to attribute to impudence, ignorance, or stupidity the idea that the difficult Latin required no other instrument than a dictionary; in order fully to undeceive him I sent the *Gradus ad Parnassum* of Quicherat, and the Pliny.

On 14 February, I received a telegram from Buenos Aires telling me to return immediately, for my father was 'in no way well.' God forgive me, but the prestige of being the recipient of an urgent telegram, the desire to point out to all of Fray Bentos the contradiction between the negative form of the news and the positive adverb, the temptation to dramatize my sorrow as I feigned a virile stoicism, all no doubt distracted me from the possibility of anguish. As I packed my valise, I noticed that I was missing the *Gradus* and the volume of the *Historia Naturalis*. The 'Saturn' was to weigh anchor on the morning of the next day; that night, after supper, I made my way to the house of Funes. Outside, I was surprised to find the night no less oppressive than the day.

Ireneo's mother received me at the modest ranch.

She told me that Ireneo was in the back room and that I should not be disturbed to find him in the dark, for he knew how to pass the dead hours without lighting the candle. I crossed the cobblestone patio, the small corridor; I came to the second patio. A great vine covered everything, so that the darkness seemed complete. Of a sudden I heard the high-pitched, mocking voice of Ireneo. The voice spoke in Latin; the voice (which came out of the obscurity) was reading, with obvious delight, a treatise or prayer or incantation. The Roman syllables resounded in the earthen patio; my suspicion made them seem undecipherable, interminable; afterwards, in the enormous dialogue of that night, I learned that they made up the first paragraph of the twenty-fourth chapter of the seventh book of the *Historia Naturalis*. The subject of this chapter is memory; the last words are *ut nihil non iisdem verbis redderetur auditum*.

Without the least change in his voice, Ireneo bade me come in. He was lying on the cot, smoking. It seems to me that I did not see his face until dawn; I seem to recall the momentary glow of the cigarette. The room smelled vaguely of dampness. I sat down, and repeated the story of the telegram and my father's illness.

I come now to the most difficult point in my narrative. For the entire story has no other point (the reader might as well know it by now) than this dialogue of almost a half-century ago. I shall not attempt to reproduce his words, now irrecoverable. I prefer truthfully to make a résumé of the many things Ireneo told me. The indirect style is remote and weak; I know that I sacrifice the effectiveness of my narrative; but let my readers imagine the nebulous sentences which clouded that night.

Ireneo began by enumerating, in Latin and Spanish, the cases of prodigious memory cited in the *Historia Naturalis*: Cyrus, king of the Persians, who could call every soldier in his armies by name; Mithridates Eupator, who administered justice in the twenty-two languages of his empire; Simonides, inventor of mnemotechny; Metrodorus, who practised the art of repeating faithfully what he heard once. With evident good faith Funes marvelled that such things should be considered marvellous. He told me that previous to the rainy afternoon when the blue-tinted horse threw him, he had been – like any Christian – blind, deaf-mute, somnambulistic, memoryless. (I tried to remind him of his precise perception of time, his memory for proper names; he paid no attention to me.) For nineteen years, he said, he had lived like a person in a dream: he looked without seeing, heard without hearing, forgot everything – almost everything. On falling from the horse, he lost consciousness; when he recovered it, the present was almost intolerable it was so rich and bright; the same was true of the most ancient and most trivial memories. A little later he realized that he was crippled. This fact scarcely interested him. He reasoned (or felt) that immobility was a minimum price to pay. And now, his perception and his memory were infallible.

We, in a glance, perceive three wine glasses on the table; Funes saw all the shoots, clusters, and grapes of the vine. He remembered the shapes of the clouds in the south at dawn on

the 30th of April of 1882, and he could compare them in his
recollection with the marbled grain in the design of a leather-
bound book which he had seen only once, and with the lines
in the spray which an oar raised in the Rio Negro on the eve of
the battle of the Quebracho. These recollections were not
simple; each visual image was linked to muscular sensations,
thermal sensations, etc. He could reconstruct all his dreams,
all his fancies. Two or three times he had reconstructed an
entire day. He told me: *I have more memories in myself alone than
all men have had since the world was a world.* And again: *My
dreams are like your vigils.* And again, toward dawn: *My
memory, sir, is like a garbage disposal.*

A circumference on a blackboard, a rectangular triangle, a
rhomb, are forms which we can fully intuit; the same held
true with Ireneo for the tempestuous mane of a stallion, a
herd of cattle in a pass, the ever-changing flame or the
innumerable ash, the many faces of a dead man during the
course of a protracted wake. He could perceive I do not know
how many stars in the sky.

These things he told me; neither then nor at any time later
did they seem doubtful. In those days neither the cinema nor
the phonograph yet existed; nevertheless, it seems strange,
almost incredible, that no one should have experimented on
Funes. The truth is that we all live by leaving behind; no
doubt we all profoundly know that we are immortal and that
sooner or later every man will do all things and know
everything.

The voice of Funes, out of the darkness, continued. He
told me that toward 1886 he had devised a new system of
enumeration and that in a very few days he had gone beyond
twenty-four thousand. He had not written it down, for what
he once meditated would not be erased. The first stimulus to
his work, I believe, had been his discontent with the fact that
'thirty-three Uruguayans' required two symbols and three
words, rather than a single word and a single symbol. Later he
applied his extravagant principle to the other numbers. In
place of seven thousand thirteen, he would say (for example)
Máximo Perez; in place of seven thousand fourteen, *The Train*;

other numbers were *Luis Melián Lafinur, Olimar, Brimstone, Clubs, The Whale, Gas, The Cauldron, Napoleon, Agustín de Vedia*. In lieu of five hundred, he would say *nine*. Each word had a particular sign, a species of mark; the last were very complicated. ... I attempted to explain that this rhapsody of unconnected terms was precisely the contrary of a system of enumeration. I said that to say three hundred and sixty-five was to say three hundreds, six tens, five units: an analysis which does not exist in such numbers as *The Negro Timoteo* or *The Flesh Blanket*. Funes did not understand me, or did not wish to understand me.

Locke, in the seventeenth century, postulated (and rejected) an impossible idiom in which each individual object, each stone, each bird and branch had an individual name; Funes had once projected an analogous idiom, but he had renounced it as being too general, too ambiguous. In effect, Funes not only remembered every leaf on every tree of every wood, but even every one of the times he had perceived or imagined it. He determined to reduce all of his past experience to some seventy thousand recollections, which he would later define numerically. Two considerations dissuaded him: the thought that the task was interminable and the thought that it was useless. He knew that at the hour of his death he would scarcely have finished classifying even all the memories of his childhood.

The two projects I have indicated (an infinite vocabulary for the natural series of numbers, and a usable mental catalogue of all the images of memory) are lacking in sense, but they reveal a certain stammering greatness. They allow us to make out dimly, or to infer, the dizzying world of Funes. He was, let us not forget, almost incapable of general, platonic ideas. It was not only difficult for him to understand that the generic term *dog* embraced so many unlike specimens of differing sizes and different forms; he was disturbed by the fact that a dog at three-fourteen (seen in profile) should have the same name as the dog at three-fifteen (seen from the front). His own face in the mirror, his own hands, surprised him on every occasion. Swift writes that the emperor of

Lilliput could discern the movement of the minute hand; Funes could continuously make out the tranquil advances of corruption, of caries, of fatigue. He noted the progress of death, of moisture. He was the solitary and lucid spectator of a multiform world which was instantaneously and almost intolerably exact. Babylon, London, and New York have overawed the imagination of men with their ferocious splendour; no one, in those populous towers or upon those surging avenues, has felt the heat and pressure of a reality as indefatigable as that which day and night converged upon the unfortunate Ireneo in his humble South American farmhouse. It was very difficult for him to sleep. To sleep is to be abstracted from the world; Funes, on his back in his cot, in the shadows, imagined every crevice and every moulding of the various houses which surrounded him. (I repeat, the least important of his recollections was more minutely precise and more lively than our perception of a physical pleasure or a physical torment.) Toward the east, in a section which was not yet cut into blocks of homes, there were some new unknown houses. Funes imagined them black, compact, made of a single obscurity; he would turn his face in this direction in order to sleep. He would also imagine himself at the bottom of the river, being rocked and annihilated by the current.

Without effort, he had learned English, French, Portuguese, Latin. I suspect, nevertheless, that he was not very capable of thought. To think is to forget a difference, to generalize, to abstract. In the overly replete world of Funes there were nothing but details, almost contiguous details.

The equivocal clarity of dawn penetrated along the earthen patio.

Then it was that I saw the face of the voice which had spoken all through the night. Ireneo was nineteen years old; he had been born in 1868; he seemed as monumental as bronze, more ancient than Egypt, anterior to the prophecies and the pyramids. It occurred to me that each one of my words (each one of my gestures) would live on in his implacable memory; I was benumbed by the fear of multiplying superfluous gestures.

Ireneo Funes died in 1889, of a pulmonary congestion.

1942   *Translated by* ANTHONY KERRIGAN

THE FORM OF THE SWORD

To E.H.M.

His face was crossed with a rancorous scar: a nearly perfect ashen arc which sank into his temple on one side and his cheek on the other. His real name is of no importance: in Tacuarembó everyone knew him as the Englishman of La Colorada. The great landowner of these parts, Cardoso, had not been interested in selling; I have heard that the Englishman had recourse to an unexpected argument: he told him the secret history of the scar. The Englishman had come from the frontier, from Rio Grande del Sur; there were those who said he had been a smuggler in Brazil. His fields were overgrown with underbrush; the wells were bitter; to remedy these faults, the Englishman worked alongside his *peones*. They say he was strict to the point of cruelty, but scrupulously fair. They also say he was a drinking man: a couple of times a year he would lock himself up in a room in the tower, and two or three days later he would emerge as if from a bout of insanity or from the battlefield, pale, tremulous, abashed – and as authoritarian as ever. I remember his glacial eyes, his energetic thinness, his grey moustache. He had scant dealings with anyone; true, his Spanish was rudimentary, contaminated with Brazilian. Apart from an occasional commercial letter or pamphlet, he received no correspondence.

The last time I made a trip through the Northern provinces a flash flood in the Caraguatá arroyo forced me to spend the night at La Colorada. I was only there a few minutes when I felt that my presence was inopportune. I tried getting into the good graces of the Englishman; I resorted to the least acute of all the passions: patriotism. I said that a country with the spirit of England was invincible. My interlocutor agreed, but he added with a smile that he was not English. He was Irish, from Dungarvan. Having said this, he stopped himself, as if he had revealed a secret.

After supper we went out to look at the sky. It had cleared, but behind the ridge of the mountains, the south, fissured and shot through with lightning flashes, was brewing up another storm. Back in the deserted dining room, the waiter who had served us supper brought out a bottle of rum. We drank steadily, in silence.

I do not know what hour of the night it might have been when I realized that I was drunk; I do not know what inspiration or exultation or tedium made me mention the scar. The Englishman's face changed colour. For a few seconds I thought he was going to ask me to leave. Finally he said, in a normal voice:

'I'll tell you the story of my wound on one condition: that you do not minimize the opprobrium it calls forth, that you not belittle a single infamous circumstance.'

I agreed. And this, then, is the story he recounted, in a mixture of English, Spanish, and Portuguese:

About 1922, in a city in Connaught, I was one of many men conspiring for Irish independence. Of my comrades, some survived to engage in peaceful pursuits; others, paradoxically, fight in the desert and at sea under the English colours; another, the man of greatest worth, died in the courtyard of a barracks, at dawn, before a firing squad of soldiers drowsy with sleep; still others (not the most unfortunate ones) met their fate in the anonymous and nearly secret battles of the civil war. We were Republicans, Catholics; we were, I suspect, romantics. For us Ireland was not only the utopian future and the intolerable present; it was a bitter and loving mythology, it was the circular towers and the red bogs, it was the repudiation of Parnell and the enormous epics which sing of the theft of bulls who in a former incarnation were heroes and in others were fish and mountains. ... On one evening I shall never forget, we were joined by a comrade from Munster: a certain John Vincent Moon.

He was scarcely twenty years old. He was thin and soft at the same time. He gave one the uncomfortable impression of being invertebrate. He had studied, with fervour and vanity, every page of some communist manual or other; dialectical materialism served him as a means to end any and all discussion. The reasons that one man may have to abominate another, or love him, are infinite: Moon reduced universal history to a sordid economic conflict. He asserted that the revolution is predestined to triumph. I told him that only lost causes can interest a gentleman. ... By then it was nighttime. We continued our disagreements along the corridor, down the stairs, into the vague streets. The judgements emitted by Moon impressed me less than their unattractive and apodictic tone. The new comrade did not argue: he passed judgement with obvious disdain and a certain fury.

As we came to the outlying houses, a sudden exchange of gunfire caught us by surprise. (Just before or after, we skirted the blank wall of a factory or barracks.) We took refuge along a dirt road; a soldier, looming gigantic in the glare, rushed out of a burning cabin. He shrieked at us and ordered us to halt. I pressed on; my comrade did not follow me. I turned back: John Vincent Moon was frozen in his tracks, fascinated and eternalized, as it were, by terror. I rushed to his side, brought down the soldier with a single blow, shook and pounded Vincent Moon, berated him, and ordered him to follow me. I was forced to yank him by his arm; a passionate fear paralysed him. We fled through a night suddenly shot through with blazes. A burst of rifle fire sought us out; a bullet grazed Moon's right shoulder; while we ran among the pines, he broke into feeble sobbing.

During that autumn of 1922 I had taken refuge in a country house belonging to General Berkeley. This officer (whom I had never seen) was carrying out some administrative assignment in Bengal. His house, though it was less than a hundred years old, was dark and deteriorated and abounded in perplexing corridors and vain antechambers. A museum and an enormous library usurped the ground floor: controversial and incompatible books which, somehow, make up the history of the nineteenth century; scimitars from Nishapur, in whose arrested circular arcs the wind and violence of battle seemed to last. We entered (I seem to remember) through the back part of the house. Moon, his lips dry and quivering, muttered that the events of the evening had been very interesting. I dressed his wound, and brought him a cup of tea. (His 'wound', I saw, was superficial.) Suddenly he stammered perplexedly:

'But you took a considerable chance.'

I told him not to worry. (The routine of the civil war had impelled me to act as I had acted. Besides, the capture of a single one of our men could have compromised our cause.)

The following day Moon had recovered his aplomb. He accepted a cigarette, and severely cross-questioned me concerning 'the economic resources of our revolutionary party'. His questions were quite lucid. I told him (in all truth) that the situation was serious. Shattering volleys of rifle fire reverberated in the south. I told Moon that our comrades expected us. My trench coat and revolver were in my room; when I returned, I found Moon stretched on the sofa, his eyes shut. He thought he had fever; he spoke of a painful shoulder spasm.

I realized then that his cowardice was irreparable. I awkwardly urged him to take care of himself and took my leave. I blushed for this fearful man, as if I, and not Vincent Moon, were the coward. What one man does is something done, in some measure, by all men. For that reason a disobedience committed in a garden contaminates the human race; for that reason it is not unjust that the crucifixion of a single Jew suffices to save it. Perhaps Schopenhauer is right: I am all others, any man is all men, Shakespeare is in some way the wretched John Vincent Moon.

We spent nine days in the enormous house of the General. Of the agony and splendour of the battle I shall say nothing: my intention is to tell the story of this scar which affronts me. In my memory, those nine days form a single day; except for the next to the last, when our men rushed a barracks and we were able to avenge, man for man, the sixteen comrades who had been machine-gunned at Elphin. I would slip out of the house towards dawn, in the confusion of the morning twilight. I was back by dusk. My companion would be waiting for me upstairs: his wound did not allow him to come down to meet me. I can see him with some book of strategy in his

hand: F.N. Maude or Clausewitz. 'The artillery is my
preferred arm,' he conceded one night. He would inquire into
our plans; he liked to censure or revamp them. He was also in
the habit of denouncing our 'deplorable economic base'.
Dogmatic and sombre, he would prophesy a ruinous end.
C'est une affaire flambée, he would murmur. In order to show
that his being a physical coward made no difference to him,
he increased his intellectual arrogance. Thus, for better or for
worse, passed nine days.

On the tenth, the city definitively fell into the hands of the
Black and Tans. Tall silent horsemen patrolled the streets.
The wind was filled with ashes and smoke. At an intersection
in the middle of a square, I saw a corpse – less tenacious in my
memory than a manikin – upon which some soldiers interminably practised their marksmanship. . . . I had left my quarters
as the sunrise hung in the sky. I returned before midday. In
the library, Moon was talking to someone; by his tone of voice
I realized that he was using the telephone. Then I heard my
name; then that I would return at seven; then the suggestion
that I be arrested as I crossed the garden. My reasonable
friend was selling me reasonably. I heard him requesting
certain guarantees of personal security.

At this point my story becomes confused, its thread is lost.
I know I pursued the informer down the dark corridors of
nightmare and the deep stairs of vertigo. Moon had come to
know the house very well, much better than I. Once or twice I
lost him. I cornered him before the soldiers arrested me.
From one of the general's mounted sets of arms I snatched
down a cutlass; with the steel half-moon I sealed his face, for
ever, with a half-moon of blood. Borges, I have confessed this
to you, a stranger. *Your* contempt will not wound me as much.

Here the narrator stopped. I noticed that his hands were
trembling.

'And Moon?' I asked him.

'He was paid the Judas-money, and fled to Brazil. And that
afternoon, he watched some drunks in an impromptu firing
squad in the town square shoot down a manikin.'

I waited in vain for him to go on with his story. At length I asked him to continue.

A sob shook his body. And then, with feeble sweetness, he pointed to the white arced scar.

'You don't believe me?' he stammered. 'Don't you see the mark of infamy written on my face? I told you the story the way I did so that you would hear it to the end. I informed on the man who took me in: I am Vincent Moon. Despise me.'

1942   *Translated by* ANTHONY KERRIGAN

THEME OF THE TRAITOR
AND HERO

So the Platonic Year
Whirls out new right and wrong
Whirls in the old instead;
All men are dancers and their tread
Goes to the barbarous clangour of a gong.
                    – W. B. Yeats, *The Tower*

Under the influence of the flagrant Chesterton (contriver and embellisher of elegant mysteries) and of the court counsellor Leibnitz (who invented pre-established harmony), I have imagined the following argument, which I shall doubtless develop (and which already justifies me in some way) on profitless afternoons. Details, revisions, adjustments are lacking; there are areas of this history which are not yet revealed to me; today, the third of January of 1944, I dimly perceive it thus:

The action transpires in some oppressed and stubborn country: Poland, Ireland, the Republic of Venice, some state in South America or the Balkans. ... *Has transpired*, we should say, for although the narrator is contemporary, the narrative related by him occurred towards the middle or beginnings of the nineteenth century. Let us say, for purposes of narration, that it was in Ireland, in 1824. The narrator is named Ryan; he is a great-grandson of the young, heroic, handsome, assassinated Fergus Kilpatrick, whose sepulchre was mysteriously violated, whose name embellishes the verse of Browning and Hugo, whose statue presides over a grey hill amidst red moors.

Kilpatrick was a conspirator, a secret and glorious captain of conspirators; he was like Moses in that, from the land of Moab, he descried the Promised Land but would not ever set foot there, for he perished on the eve of the victorious rebellion which he had premeditated and conjured. The date

of the first centenary of his death draws near; the circumstances of the crime are enigmatic; Ryan, engaged in compil-
ing a biography of the hero, discovers that the enigma goes
beyond the purely criminal. Kilpatrick was assassinated in a
theatre; the English police could find no trace of the killer;
historians declare that the failure of the police does not in any
way impugn their good intentions, for he was no doubt killed
by order of this same police. Other phases of the enigma
disquiet Ryan. These facets are of cyclic character: they seem
to repeat or combine phenomena from remote regions, from
remote ages. Thus, there is no one who does not know that
the bailiffs who examined the hero's cadaver discovered a
sealed letter which warned him of the risk of going to the
theatre on that particular night: Julius Caesar, too, as he
walked towards the place where the knives of his friends
awaited him, was handed a message, which he never got to the
point of reading, in which the treason was declared, and the
names of the traitors given. In her dreams, Caesar's wife,
Calpurnia, saw a tower, which the Senate had dedicated to
her husband, fallen to the ground; false and anonymous
rumours throughout the land were occasioned, on the eve of
Kilpatrick's death, by the burning of the round tower of
Kilgarvan – an event which might have seemed an omen,
since Kilpatrick had been born at Kilgarvan. These parallels
(and others) in the history of Caesar and the history of an
Irish conspirator induce Ryan to assume a secret pattern in
time, a drawing in which the lines repeat themselves. He
ponders the decimal history imagined by Condorcet; the
morphologies proposed by Hegel, Spengler, and Vico; the
characters of Hesiod, who degenerate from gold to iron. He
considers the transmigration of souls, a doctrine which
horrifies Celtic belles-lettres and which the very same Caesar
attributed to the Britannic Druids; he thinks that before the
hero was Fergus Kilpatrick, Fergus Kilpatrick was Julius
Caesar. From these circular labyrinths he is saved by a
curious species of proof which immediately plunges him into
other labyrinths even more inextricable and heterogeneous:
certain words spoken by a mendicant who conversed with

Fergus Kilpatrick on the day of his death were prefigured in the tragedy of Macbeth. That history should have imitated history was already sufficiently marvellous; that history should imitate literature is inconceivable. . . .

Ryan discovers that in 1814, James Alexander Nolan, the oldest of the hero's comrades, had translated into Gaelic the principal dramas of Shakespeare, among them *Julius Caesar*. In the archives he also finds a manuscript article by Nolan on *Festspiele* of Switzerland: vast and roving theatrical representations these, which require thousands of actors and which reiterate historic episodes in the same cities and mountains where they occurred. Still another unpublished document reveals that a few days before the end, Kilpatrick, presiding over his last conclave, had signed the death sentence of a traitor, whose name has been blotted out. This sentence scarcely harmonizes with Kilpatrick's pious attitude. Ryan goes deeper into the matter (the investigation covers one of the hiatuses in the argument) and he succeeds in solving the enigma.

Kilpatrick was brought to his end in a theatre, but he made of the entire city a theatre, too, and the actors were legion. And the drama which was climaxed by his death embraced many days and many nights. Here is what happened:

On the second of August of 1824, the conspirators gathered. The country was ripe for rebellion. But somehow every attempt always failed: there was a traitor in the group. Fergus Kilpatrick ordered James Nolan to uncover this traitor. Nolan carried out his orders: before the gathering as a whole, he announced that the traitor was Kilpatrick himself. He demonstrated the truth of his accusation with irrefutable proofs; the conspirators condemned their president to death. The latter signed his own death sentence; but he implored that his condemnation not be allowed to hurt the fatherland.

Nolan thereupon conceived his strange project. Ireland idolized Kilpatrick; the most tenuous suspicion of his disgrace would have compromised the rebellion; Nolan proposed a plan which would make Kilpatrick's execution an instrument for the liberation of the fatherland. He suggested the condemned man die at the hands of an unknown assassin, in circumstances deliberately dramatic, which would engrave themselves upon the popular imagination and which would speed the revolt. Kilpatrick swore to collaborate in a project which allowed him the opportunity to redeem himself and which would add a flourish to his death.

Pressed for time, Nolan was unable to integrate the circumstances he invented for the complex execution; he was forced to plagiarize another dramatist, the enemy-Englishman William Shakespeare. He repeated scenes from *Macbeth*, and from *Julius Caesar*. The public – and the secret – presentation took several days. The condemned man entered Dublin, discussed, worked, prayed, reproved, spoke words which seemed (later) to be pathetic – and each one of these acts, which would eventually be glorious, had been foreordained by Nolan. Hundreds of actors collaborated with the protagonist; the role of some was stellar, that of others ephemeral. What they said and did remains in the books of history, in the impassioned memory of Ireland. Kilpatrick, carried away by the minutely scrupulous destiny which redeemed and condemned him, more than once enriched the text (Nolan's text) with words and deeds of his own improvisation. And thus did the popular drama unfold in Time, until, on the sixth of August of 1824, in a theatre box hung with funereal curtains, which foreshadowed Abraham Lincoln's, the anticipated pistol-shot entered the breast of the traitor and hero, who could scarcely articulate, between two effusions of violent blood, some prearranged words.

In Nolan's work, the passages imitated from Shakespeare are the *least* dramatic; Ryan suspects that the author interpolated them so that one person, in the future, might realize the truth. He understands that he, too, forms part of Nolan's plan. ... At the end of some tenacious cavilling, he resolves to keep silent his discovery. He publishes a book dedicated to the glory of the hero; this too, no doubt, was foreseen.

Translated by ANTHONY KERRIGAN

DEATH AND THE COMPASS

To Mandie Molina Vedia

Of the many problems which exercised the daring perspicac-
ity of Lönnrot none was so strange – so harshly strange, we
may say – as the staggered series of bloody acts which
culminated at the villa of Triste-le-Roy, amid the boundless
odour of the eucalypti. It is true that Erik Lönnrot did not
succeed in preventing the last crime, but it is indisputable
that he foresaw it. Nor did he, of course, guess the identity of
Yarmolinsky's unfortunate assassin, but he did divine the
secret morphology of the vicious series as well as the participation of Red Scharlach, whose alias is Scharlach the Dandy.
This criminal (as so many others) had sworn on his honour to
kill Lönnrot, but the latter had never allowed himself to be
intimidated. Lönnrot thought of himself as a pure thinker, an
Auguste Dupin, but there was something of the adventurer in
him; and even of the gamester.

The first crime occurred at the Hôtel du Nord – that high
prism that dominates the estuary whose waters are the colours
of the desert. To this tower (which most manifestly unites the
hateful whiteness of a sanatorium, the numbered divisibility
of a prison, and the general appearance of a bawdy house) on
the third day of December came the delegate from Podolsk to
the Third Talmudic Congress, Doctor Marcel Yarmolinsky, a
man of grey beard and grey eyes. We shall never know
whether the Hôtel du Nord pleased him: he accepted it with
the ancient resignation which had allowed him to endure
three years of war in the Carpathians and three thousand
years of oppression and pogroms. He was given a sleeping
room on floor R, in front of the suite which the Tetrarch of
Galilee occupied not without some splendour. Yarmolinsky
supped, postponed until the following day an investigation of
the unknown city, arranged upon a cupboard his many books
and his few possessions, and before midnight turned off the
light. (Thus declared the Tetrarch's chauffeur, who slept in

an adjoining room.) On the fourth, at 11.03 a.m., there was a telephone call for him from the editor of the *Yiddische Zeitung*; Doctor Yarmolinsky did not reply; he was found in his room, his face already a little dark, and his body almost nude, beneath a large anachronistic cape. He was lying not far from the door which gave on to the corridor; a deep stab wound had split open his breast. In the same room, a couple of hours later, in the midst of journalists, photographers, and police, Commissioner Treviranus and Lönnrot were discussing the problem with equanimity.

'There's no need to look for a Chimera, or a cat with three legs,' Treviranus was saying as he brandished an imperious cigar. 'We all know that the Tetrarch of Galilee is the possessor of the finest sapphires in the world. Someone, intending to steal them, came in here by mistake. Yarmolinsky got up; the robber had to kill him. What do you think?'

'It's possible, but not interesting,' Lönnrot answered. 'You will reply that reality hasn't the slightest need to be of interest. And I'll answer you that reality may avoid the obligation to be interesting, but that hypotheses may not. In the hypothesis you have postulated, chance intervenes largely. Here lies a dead rabbi; I should prefer a purely rabbinical explanation, not the imaginary mischances of an imaginary robber.'

Treviranus answered ill-humouredly:

'I am not interested in rabbinical explanations; I am interested in the capture of the man who stabbed this unknown person.'

'Not so unknown,' corrected Lönnrot. 'Here are his complete works.' He indicated a line of tall volumes: *A Vindication of the Cabala*; *An Examination of the Philosophy of Robert Fludd*; a literal translation of the *Sepher Yezirah*; a *Biography of the Baal Shem*; a *History of the Sect of the Hasidim*; a monograph (in German) on the Tetragrammaton; another, on the divine nomenclature of the Pentateuch. The Commissioner gazed at them with suspicion, almost with revulsion. Then he fell to laughing.

'I'm only a poor Christian,' he replied. 'Carry off all these moth-eaten classics if you like; I haven't got time to lose in Jewish superstitions.'

'Maybe this crime belongs to the history of Jewish superstitions,' murmured Lönnrot.

'Like Christianity,' the editor of the *Yiddische Zeitung* dared to put in. He was a myope, an atheist, and very timid.

No one answered him. One of the agents had found inserted in the small typewriter a piece of paper on which was written the following inconclusive sentence.

The first letter of the Name has been spoken

Lönnrot abstained from smiling. Suddenly become a bibliophile – or Hebraist – he directed that the dead man's books be made into a parcel, and he carried them to his office. Indifferent to the police investigation, he dedicated himself to studying them. A large octavo volume revealed to him the teachings of Israel Baal Shem-Tob, founder of the sect of the Pious; another volume, the virtues and terrors of the Tetragrammaton, which is the ineffable name of God; another, the thesis that God has a secret name, in which is epitomized (as in the crystal sphere which the Persians attribute to Alexander of Macedon) his ninth attribute, eternity – that is to say, the immediate knowledge of everything that will exist, exists, and has existed in the universe. Tradition numbers ninety-nine names of God; the Hebraists attribute this imperfect number to the magical fear of even numbers; the Hasidim reason that this hiatus indicates a hundredth name – the Absolute Name.

From this erudition he was distracted, within a few days, by the appearance of the editor of the *Yiddische Zeitung*. This man wished to talk of the assassination; Lönnrot preferred to speak of the diverse names of God. The journalist declared, in three columns, that the investigator Erik Lönnrot had dedicated himself to studying the names of God in order to 'come up with' the name of the assassin. Lönnrot, habituated to the simplifications of journalism, did not become indignant. One of those shopkeepers who have found that there are buyers for every book came out with a popular edition of the *History of the Sect of the Hasidim.*

The second crime occurred on the night of the third of January, in the most deserted and empty corner of the capital's western suburbs. Towards dawn, one of the gendarmes who patrol these lonely places on horseback detected a man in a cape, lying prone in the shadow of an ancient paint shop. The hard visage seemed bathed in blood; a deep stab wound had split open his breast. On the wall, upon the yellow and red rhombs, there were some words written in chalk. The gendarme spelled them out. . . .

That afternoon Treviranus and Lönnrot made their way towards the remote scene of the crime. To the left and right of the automobile, the city disintegrated; the firmament grew larger and the houses meant less and less and a brick kiln or a poplar grove more and more. They reached their miserable destination: a final alley of rose-coloured mud walls which in some way seemed to reflect the disordered setting of the sun. The dead man had already been identified. He was Daniel Simon Azevedo, a man of some fame in the ancient northern suburbs, who had risen from wagoner to political tough, only to degenerate later into a thief and even an informer. (The singular style of his death struck them as appropriate: Azevedo was the last representative of a generation of bandits who knew how to handle a dagger, but not a revolver.) The words in chalk were the following:

The second letter of the Name has been spoken

The third crime occurred on the night of the third of February. A little before one o'clock, the telephone rang in the office of Commissioner Treviranus. In avid secretiveness a man with a guttural voice spoke: he said his name was Ginzberg (or Ginsburg) and that he was disposed to communicate, for a reasonable remuneration, an explanation of the two sacrifices of Azevedo and Yarmolinsky. The discordant sound of whistles and horns drowned out the voice of the informer. Then the connexion was cut off. Without rejecting the possibility of a hoax (it was carnival time), Treviranus checked and found he had been called from Liverpool House, a tavern on the Rue de Toulon – that dirty street where cheek by jowl are the peepshow and the milk store, the bordello and the women selling Bibles. Treviranus called back and spoke to the owner. This personage (Black Finnegan by name, an old Irish criminal who was crushed, annihilated almost, by respectability) told him that the last person to use the establishment's phone had been a lodger, a certain Gryphius, who had just gone out with some friends. Treviranus immediately went to Liverpool House, where Finnegan related the following facts. Eight days previously, Gryphius had taken a room above the saloon. He was a man of sharp features, a nebulous grey beard, shabbily clothed in black; Finnegan (who put the room to a use which Treviranus guessed) demanded a rent which was undoubtedly excessive; Gryphius immediately paid the stipulated sum. He scarcely ever went out; he dined and lunched in his room; his face was hardly known in the bar. On this particular night, he came down to telephone from Finnegan's office. A closed coupé stopped in front of the tavern. The driver did not move from his seat; several of the patrons recalled that he was wearing a bear mask. Two harlequins descended from the coupé; they were short in stature, and no one could fail to observe that they were very drunk. With a tooting of horns they burst into Finnegan's office; they embraced Gryphius, who seemed to recognize them but who replied to them coldly; they exchanged a few words in Yiddish – he, in a low guttural voice; they, in shrill, falsetto tones – and then the party climbed to the upstairs room. Within a quarter hour the three descended, very joyous; Gryphius, staggering, seemed as drunk as the others. He walked – tall, dazed – in the middle, between the masked harlequins. (One of the women in the bar remembered the yellow, red, and green rhombs, the diamond designs.) Twice he stumbled; twice he was held up by the harlequins. Alongside the adjoining dock basin, whose water was rectangular, the trio got into the coupé and disappeared. From the running board, the last of the harlequins had scrawled an obscene figure and a sentence on one of the slates of the outdoor shed.

Treviranus gazed upon the sentence. It was nearly foreknowable. It read:

The last of the letters of the Name has been spoken

He examined, then, the small room of Gryphius-Ginzberg. On the floor was a violent star of blood; in the corners, the remains of some Hungarian-brand cigarettes; in a cabinet, a book in Latin – the *Philologus Hebraeo-Graecus* (1739) of Leusden – along with various manuscript notes. Treviranus studied the book with indignation and had Lönnrot summoned. The latter, without taking off his hat, began to read while the Commissioner questioned the contradictory witnesses to the possible kidnapping. At four in the morning they came out. In the tortuous Rue de Toulon, as they stepped on the dead serpentines of the dawn, Treviranus said:

'And supposing the story of this night were a sham?'

Erik Lönnrot smiled and read him with due gravity a passage (underlined) of the thirty-third dissertation of the *Philologus*:

Dies Judaeorum incipit a solis occasu
usque ad solis occasum diei sequentis.

'This means,' he added, 'that *the Hebrew day begins at sundown and lasts until the following sundown.*'

Treviranus attempted an irony.

'Is this fact the most worthwhile you've picked up tonight?'

'No. Of even greater value is a word Ginzberg used.'

The afternoon dailies did not neglect this series of disappearances. *The Cross and the Sword* contrasted them with the admirable discipline and order of the last Eremitical Congress; Ernest Palast, writing in *The Martyr*, spoke out against 'the intolerable delays in this clandestine and frugal pogrom, which has taken three months to liquidate three Jews'; the *Yiddische Zeitung* rejected the terrible hypothesis of an anti-

Semitic plot, 'even though many discerning intellects do not admit of any other solution to the triple mystery'; the most illustrious gunman in the South, Dandy Red Scharlach, swore that in his district such crimes as these would never occur, and he accused Commissioner Franz Treviranus of criminal negligence.

On the night of March first, the Commissioner received an imposing-looking, sealed envelope. He opened it: the envelope contained a letter signed Baruj Spinoza, and a detailed plan of the city, obviously torn from a Baedeker. The letter prophesied that on the third of March there would *not* be a fourth crime, inasmuch as the paint shop in the West, the Tavern on the Rue de Toulon and the Hôtel du Nord were the 'perfect vertices of an equilateral and mystic triangle'; the regularity of this triangle was made clear on the map with red ink. This argument, *more geometrico*, Treviranus read with resignation, and sent the letter and map on to Lönnrot – who deserved such a piece of insanity.

Erik Lönnrot studied the documents. The three sites were in fact equidistant. Symmetry in time (the third of December, the third of January, the third of February); symmetry in space as well. ... Of a sudden he sensed he was about to decipher the mystery. A set of calipers and a compass completed his sudden intuition. He smiled, pronounced the word 'Tetragrammaton' (of recent acquisition), and called the Commissioner on the telephone. He told him:

'Thank you for the equilateral triangle you sent me last night. It has enabled me to solve the problem. Tomorrow, Friday, the criminals will be in jail, we can rest assured.'

'In that case, they're not planning a fourth crime?'

'Precisely because they *are* planning a fourth crime can we rest assured.'

Lönnrot hung up. An hour later he was travelling in one of the trains of the Southern Railways, en route to the abandoned villa of Triste-le-Roy. South of the city of our story there flows a blind little river filled with muddy water made disgraceful by floating scraps and garbage. On the further side is a manufacturing suburb where, under the protection of a chief from Barcelona, gunmen flourish. Lönnrot smiled to himself to think that the most famous of them – Red Scharlach – would have given anything to know of this clandestine visit. Azevedo had been a comrade of Scharlach's; Lönnrot considered the remote possibility that the fourth victim might be Scharlach himself. Then, he put aside the thought. ... He had virtually deciphered the problem; the mere circumstances, or the reality (names, prison records, faces, judicial, and penal proceedings), scarcely interested him now. Most of all he wanted to take a stroll, to relax from three months of sedentary investigation. He reflected on how the explanation of the crimes lay in an anonymous triangle and a dust-laden Greek word. The mystery seemed to him almost crystalline now; he was mortified to have dedicated a hundred days to it.

The train stopped at a silent loading platform. Lönnrot descended. It was one of those deserted afternoons which seem like dawn. The air over the muddy plain was damp and cold. Lönnrot set off across the fields. He saw dogs, he saw a wagon on a dead road, he saw the horizon, he saw a silvery horse drinking the crapulous water of a puddle. Dusk was falling when he saw the rectangular belvedere of the villa of Triste-le-Roy, almost as tall as the black eucalypti which surrounded it. He thought of the fact that only one more dawn and one more nightfall (an ancient splendour in the east, and another in the west) separated him from the hour so much desired by the seekers of the Name.

A rust coloured wrought-iron fence defined the irregular perimeter of the villa. The main gate was closed. Without much expectation of entering, Lönnrot made a complete circuit. In front of the insurmountable gate once again, he put his hand between the bars almost mechanically and chanced upon the bolt. The creaking of the iron surprised him. With laborious passivity the entire gate gave way.

Lönnrot advanced among the eucalypti, stepping amidst confused generations of rigid, broken leaves. Close up, the house on the estate of Triste-le-Roy was seen to abound in superfluous symmetries and in maniacal repetitions: a glacial

Diana in one lugubrious niche was complemented by another
Diana in another niche; one balcony was repeated by another
balcony; double steps of stairs opened into a double balus-
trade. A two-faced Hermes cast a monstrous shadow. Lönnrot circled the house as he had the estate. He examined
everything; beneath the level of the terrace he noticed a
narrow shutter door.

He pushed against it: some marble steps descended to a
vault. Versed now in the architect's preferences, Lönnrot
divined that there would be a set of stairs on the opposite wall.
He found them, ascended, raised his hands, and pushed up a
trap door.

The diffusion of light guided him to a window. He opened
it: a round, yellow moon outlined two stopped-up fountains
in the melancholy garden. Lönnrot explored the house. He
travelled through antechambers and galleries to emerge upon
duplicate patios; several times he emerged upon the same
patio. He ascended dust-covered stairways and came out into
circular antechambers; he was infinitely reflected in opposing
mirrors; he grew weary of opening or half-opening windows
which revealed the same desolate garden outside, from
various heights and various angles; inside, the furniture was
wrapped in yellow covers and the chandeliers bound up with
cretonne. A bedroom detained him; in the bedroom, a single
rose in a porcelain vase – at the first touch the ancient petals
fell apart. On the second floor, on the top storey, the house
seemed to be infinite and growing. *The house is not this large*, he
thought. *It is only made larger by the penumbra, the symmetry, the
mirrors, the years, my ignorance, the solitude.*

Going up a spiral staircase he arrived at the observatory.
The evening moon shone through the rhomboid diamonds of
the windows, which were yellow, red, and green. He was
brought to a halt by a stunning and dizzying recollection.

Two men of short stature, ferocious and stocky, hurled
themselves upon him and took his weapon. Another man,
very tall, saluted him gravely, and said:

'You are very thoughtful. You've saved us a night and a
day.'

It was Red Scharlach. His men manacled Lönnrot's hands. Lönnrot at length found his voice.

'Are you looking for the Secret Name, Scharlach?'

Scharlach remained standing, indifferent. He had not participated in the short struggle; he scarcely stretched out his hand to receive Lönnrot's revolver. He spoke; in his voice Lönnrot detected a fatigued triumph, a hatred the size of the universe, a sadness no smaller than that hatred.

'No,' answered Scharlach. 'I am looking for something more ephemeral and slippery, I am looking for Erik Lönnrot. Three years ago, in a gambling house on the Rue de Toulon, you arrested my brother and had him sent to prison. In the exchange of shots that night my men got me away in a coupé, with a police bullet in my chest. Nine days and nine nights I lay dying in this desolate, symmetrical villa; I was racked with fever, and the odious double-faced Janus who gazes towards the twilights of dusk and dawn terrorized my dreams and my waking. I learned to abominate my body, I came to feel that two eyes, two hands, two lungs are as monstrous as two faces. An Irishman attempted to convert me to the faith of Jesus; he repeated to me that famous axiom of the *goyim*: All roads lead to Rome. At night, my delirium nurtured itself on this metaphor: I sensed that the world was a labyrinth, from which it was impossible to flee, for all paths, whether they seemed to lead north or south, actually led to Rome, which was also the quadrilateral jail where my brother was dying and the villa of Triste-le-Roy. During those nights I swore by the god who sees from two faces, and by all the gods of fever and of mirrors, to weave a labyrinth around the man who had imprisoned my brother. I have woven it, and it holds: the materials are a dead writer on heresies, a compass, an eighteenth-century sect, a Greek word, a dagger, the rhombs of a paint shop.

'The first objective in the sequence was given me by chance. I had made plans with some colleagues – among them, Daniel Azevedo – to take the Tetrarch's sapphires. Azevedo betrayed us; with the money we advanced him he got himself inebriated and started on the job a day early. In the

vastness of the hotel he got lost; at two in the morning he
blundered into Yarmolinsky's room. The latter, harassed by
insomnia, had set himself to writing. He was editing some
notes, apparently, or writing an article on the Name of God;
he had just written the words *The first letter of the Name has
been spoken*. Azevedo enjoined him to be quiet; Yarmolinsky
reached out his hand for the bell which would arouse all the
hotel's forces; Azevedo at once stabbed him in the chest. It
was almost a reflex action: half a century of violence had
taught him that it was easiest and surest to kill. . . . Ten days
later, I learned through the *Yiddische Zeitung* that you were
perusing the writings of Yarmolinsky for the key to his death.
For my part I read the *History of the Sect of the Hasidim*; I
learned that the reverent fear of pronouncing the Name of
God had given rise to the doctrine that this Name is all-
powerful and mystic. I learned that some Hasidim, in search
of this secret Name, had gone as far as to offer human
sacrifices. . . . I knew you would conjecture that the Hasidim
had sacrificed the rabbi; I set myself to justifying this
conjecture.

'Marcel Yarmolinsky died on the night of December third;
for the second sacrifice I selected the night of January third.
Yarmolinsky died in the North; for the second sacrifice a place
in the West was preferable. Daniel Azevedo was the inevitable
victim. He deserved death: he was an impulsive person, a
traitor; his capture could destroy the entire plan. One of our
men stabbed him; in order to link his corpse to the other one I
wrote on the paint shop diamonds *The second letter of the Name
has been spoken*.

'The third "crime" was produced on the third of February. It was as Treviranus must have guessed, a mere mockery,
a simulacrum. I am Gryphius-Ginzberg-Ginsburg; I endured
an interminable week (filled out with a tenuous false beard) in
that perverse cubicle on the Rue de Toulon, until my friends
spirited me away. From the running board one of them wrote
on a pillar *The last of the letters of the Name has been spoken*. This
sentence revealed that the series of crimes was *triple*. And the
public thus understood it; nevertheless, I interspersed

repeated signs that would allow you, Erik Lönnrot, the reasoner, to understand that it is *quadruple*. A portent in the North, others in the East and West, demand a fourth portent in the South; the Tetragrammaton – the name of God, JHVH – is made up of *four* letters; the harlequins and the paint shop sign suggested four points. In the manual of Leusden I underlined a certain passage: it manifested that the Hebrews calculate a day counting from dusk to dusk and that therefore the death occurred on the *fourth* day of each month. To Treviranus I sent the equilateral triangle. I sensed that you would supply the missing point. The point which would form a perfect rhomb, the point which fixes where death, exactly, awaits you. In order to attract you I have premeditated everything, Erik Lönnrot, so as to draw you to the solitude of Triste-le-Roy.'

Lönnrot avoided Scharlach's eyes. He was looking at the trees and the sky divided into rhombs of turbid yellow, green, and red. He felt a little cold, and felt, too, an impersonal, almost anonymous sadness. It was already night; from the dusty garden arose the useless cry of a bird. For the last time, Lönnrot considered the problem of symmetrical and periodic death.

'In your labyrinth there are three lines too many,' he said at last. 'I know of a Greek labyrinth which is a single straight line. Along this line so many philosophers have lost themselves that a mere detective might well do so too. Scharlach, when, in some other incarnation, you hunt me, feign to commit (or do commit) a crime at A, then a second crime at B, eight kilometres from A, then a third crime at C, four kilometres from A and B, half-way en route between the two. Wait for me later at D, two kilometres from A and C, half-way, once again, between both. Kill me at D, as you are now going to kill me at Triste-le-Roy.'

'The next time I kill you,' said Scharlach, 'I promise you the labyrinth made of the single straight line which is invisible and everlasting.'

He stepped back a few paces. Then, very carefully, he fired.

1942   *Translated by* ANTHONY KERRIGAN

THE SECRET MIRACLE

> And God made him die during the
> course of a hundred years and then
> He revived him and said:
> 'How long have you been here?'
> 'A day, or part of a day,' he
> replied.
>
> *The Koran*, II, 261

On the night of 4 March 1939, in an apartment on the Zelternergasse in Prague, Jaromir Hladík, author of the unfinished tragedy *The Enemies*, of a *Vindication of Eternity*, and of an inquiry into the indirect Jewish sources of Jakob Boehme, dreamt a long drawn out chess game. The antagonists were not two individuals, but two illustrious families. The contest had begun many centuries before. No one could any longer describe the forgotten prize, but it was rumoured that it was enormous and perhaps infinite. The pieces and the chessboard were set up in a secret tower. Jaromir (in his dream) was the first-born of one of the contending families. The hour for the next move, which could not be postponed, struck on all the clocks. The dreamer ran across the sands of a rainy desert – and he could not remember the chessmen or the rules of chess. At this point he awoke. The din of the rain and the clangor of the terrible clocks ceased. A measured unison, sundered by voices of command, arose from the Zelternergasse. Day had dawned, and the armoured vanguards of the Third Reich were entering Prague.

On the 19th, the authorities received an accusation against Jaromir Hladík; on the same day, at dusk, he was arrested. He was taken to a barracks, aseptic and white, on the opposite bank of the Moldau. He was unable to refute a single one of the charges made by the Gestapo: his maternal surname was Jaroslavski, his blood was Jewish, his study of Boehme was Judaizing, his signature had helped to swell the final census of those protesting the *Anschluss*. In 1928, he had translated the *Sepher Yezirah* for the publishing house of Hermann Barsdorf; the effusive catalogue issued by this firm had exaggerated, for commercial reasons, the translator's renown; this catalogue was leafed through by Julius Rothe, one of the officials in whose hands lay Hladík's fate. The man does not exist who, outside his own specialty, is not credulous: two or three adjectives in Gothic script sufficed to convince Julius Rothe of Hladík's pre-eminence, and of the need for the death penalty, *pour encourager les autres*. The execution was set for the 29th of March, at nine in the morning. This delay (whose importance the reader will appreciate later) was due to a desire on the part of the authorities to act slowly and impersonally, in the manner of planets or vegetables.

Hladík's first reaction was simply one of horror. He was sure he would not have been terrified by the gallows, the block, or the knife; but to die before a firing squad was unbearable. In vain he repeated to himself that the pure and general act of dying, not the concrete circumstances, was the dreadful fact. He did not grow weary of imagining these circumstances: he absurdly tried to exhaust all the variations. He infinitely anticipated the process, from the sleepless dawn to the mysterious discharge of the rifles. Before the day set by Julius Rothe, he died hundreds of deaths, in courtyards whose shapes and angles defied geometry, shot down by changeable soldiers whose number varied and who sometimes put an end to him from close up and sometimes from far away. He faced these imaginary executions with true terror (perhaps with true courage). Each simulacrum lasted a few seconds. Once the circle was closed, Jaromir returned interminably to the tremulous eve of his death. Then he would reflect that reality does not tend to coincide with forecasts about it. With perverse logic he inferred that to foresee a circumstantial detail is to prevent its happening. Faithful to this feeble magic, he would invent, *so that they might not happen*, the most atrocious particulars. Naturally, he finished by fearing that these particulars were prophetic. During his wretched nights he strove to hold fast somehow to the fugitive substance of time. He knew that time was precipitating itself towards the dawn of the 29th. He reasoned aloud: *I am now in the night of the 22nd. While this night lasts (and for six more nights to come) I am invulnerable, immortal.* His nights of sleep seemed to him deep dark pools into which he might submerge. Sometimes he yearned impatiently for the firing squad's definitive volley, which would redeem him, for better or for worse, from the vain compulsion of his imagination. On the 28th, as the final sunset reverberated across the high barred windows, he was distracted from all these abject considerations by thoughts of his drama, *The Enemies.*

Hladík was past forty. Apart from a few friendships and many habits, the problematic practice of literature constituted his life. Like every writer, he measured the virtues of other writers by their performance, and asked that they measure him by what he conjectured or planned. All of the books he had published merely moved him to a complex repentance. His investigation of the work of Boehme, of Ibn Ezra, and of Fludd was essentially a product of mere application; his translation of the *Sepher Yezirah* was characterized by negligence, fatigue, and conjecture. He judged his *Vindication of Eternity* to be perhaps less deficient: the first volume is a history of the diverse eternities devised by man, from the immutable Being of Parmenides to the alterable past of Hinton; the second volume denies (with Francis Bradley) that all the events in the universe make up a temporal series. He argues that the number of experiences possible to man is not infinite, and that a single 'repetition' suffices to demonstrate that time is a fallacy. ... Unfortunately, the arguments that demonstrate this fallacy are not any less fallacious. Hladík was in the habit of running through these arguments with a certain disdainful perplexity. He had also written a series of expressionist poems; these, to the discomfiture of the author, were included in an anthology in 1924, and there was no anthology of later date which did not inherit them. Hladík was anxious to redeem himself from his equivocal and languid past with his verse drama, *The Enemies.* (He favoured the verse form in the theatre because it prevents the spectators from forgetting unreality, which is the necessary condition of art.)

This opus preserved the dramatic unities (time, place, and action). It transpires in Hradcany, in the library of the Baron Roemerstadt, on one of the last evenings of the nineteenth century. In the first scene of the first act, a stranger pays a visit to Roemerstadt. (A clock strikes seven, the vehemence of a setting sun glorifies the window panes, the air transmits familiar and impassioned Hungarian music.) This visit is followed by others; Roemerstadt does not know the people who come to importune him, but he has the uncomfortable impression that he has seen them before: perhaps in a dream. All the visitors fawn upon him, but it is obvious – first to the spectators of the drama, and then to the Baron himself – that they are secret enemies, sworn to ruin him. Roemerstadt manages to outwit, or evade, their complex intrigues. In the course of the dialogue, mention is made of his betrothed, Julia de Weidenau, and of a certain Jaroslav Kubin, who at one time had been her suitor. Kubin has now lost his mind and thinks he is Roemerstadt. ... The dangers multiply. Roemerstadt, at the end of the second act, is forced to kill one of the conspirators. The third and final act begins. The incongruities gradually mount up: actors who seemed to have been discarded from the play reappear; the man who had been killed by Roemerstadt returns, for an instant. Someone notes that the time of day has not advanced: the clock strikes seven, the western sun reverberates in the high window panes, impassioned Hungarian music is carried on the air. The first speaker in the play reappears and repeats the words he had spoken in the first scene of the first act. Roemerstadt addresses him without the least surprise. The spectator understands that Roemerstadt is the wretched Jaroslav Kubin. The drama has never taken place: it is the circular delirium which Kubin unendingly lives and relives.

Hladík had never asked himself whether this tragi-comedy of errors was preposterous or admirable, deliberate or casual. Such a plot, he intuited, was the most appropriate invention to conceal his defects and to manifest his strong points, and it embodied the possibility of redeeming (symbolically) the fundamental meaning of his life. He had already completed the first act and a scene or two of the third. The metrical nature of the work allowed him to go over it continually, rectifying the hexameters, without recourse to the manuscript. He thought of the two acts still to do, and of his coming death. In the darkness, he addressed himself to God. *If I exist at all, if I am not one of Your repetitions and errata, I exist as the author of* The Enemies. *In order to bring this drama, which may serve to justify me, to justify You, I need one more year. Grant me that year, You to whom belong the centuries and all time.* It was the last, the most atrocious night, but ten minutes later sleep swept over him like a dark ocean and drowned him.

Towards dawn, he dreamt he had hidden himself in one of the naves of the Clementine Library. A librarian wearing dark glasses asked him: *What are you looking for?* Hladík answered: *God.* The Librarian told him: *God is in one of the letters on one of the pages of one of the 400,000 volumes of the Clementine. My fathers and the fathers of my fathers have sought after that letter. I've gone blind looking for it.* He removed his glasses, and Hladík saw that his eyes were dead. A reader came in to return an atlas. *This atlas is useless,* he said, and handed it to Hladík, who opened it at random. As if through a haze, he saw a map of India. With a sudden rush of assurance, he touched one of the tiniest letters. An ubiquitous voice said: *The time for your work has been granted.* Hladík awoke.

He remembered that the dreams of men belong to God, and that Maimonides wrote that the words of a dream are divine, when they are all separate and clear and are spoken by someone invisible. He dressed. Two soldiers entered his cell and ordered him to follow them.

From behind the door, Hladík had visualized a labyrinth of passageways, stairs, and connecting blocks. Reality was less rewarding: the party descended to an inner courtyard by a single iron stairway. Some soldiers – uniforms unbuttoned – were testing a motor-cycle and disputing their conclusions. The sergeant looked at his watch: it was 8.44. They must wait until nine. Hladík, more insignificant than pitiful, sat down on a pile of firewood. He noticed that the soldiers' eyes avoided his. To make his wait easier, the sergeant offered him a cigarette. Hladík did not smoke. He accepted the cigarette out of politeness or humility. As he lit it, he saw that his hands shook. The day was clouding over. The soldiers spoke in low tones, as though he were already dead. Vainly, he strove to recall the woman of whom Julia de Weidenau was the symbol. . . .

The firing squad fell in and was brought to attention. Hladík, standing against the barracks wall, waited for the volley. Someone expressed fear the wall would be splashed with blood. The condemned man was ordered to step forward a few paces. Hladík recalled, absurdly, the preliminary manoeuvres of a photographer. A heavy drop of rain grazed one of Hladík's temples and slowly rolled down his cheek. The sergeant barked the final command.

The physical universe stood still.

The rifles converged upon Hladík, but the men assigned to pull the triggers were immobile. The sergeant's arm eternalized an inconclusive gesture. Upon a courtyard flagstone a bee cast a stationary shadow. The wind had halted, as in a painted picture. Hladík began a shriek, a syllable, a twist of the hand. He realized he was paralysed. Not a sound reached him from the stricken world.

He thought: *I'm in hell, I'm dead*.

He thought: *I've gone mad*.

He thought: *Time has come to a halt*.

Then he reflected that in that case, his thought, too, would have come to a halt. He was anxious to test this possibility: he repeated (without moving his lips) the mysterious Fourth Eclogue of Virgil. He imagined that the already remote soldiers shared his anxiety; he longed to communicate with them. He was astonished that he felt no fatigue, no vertigo from his protracted immobility. After an indeterminate length of time he fell asleep. On awaking he found the world still motionless and numb. The drop of water still clung to his cheek; the shadow of the bee still did not shift in the courtyard; the smoke from the cigarette he had thrown away did not blow away. Another 'day' passed before Hladík understood.

He had asked God for an entire year in which to finish his work: His omnipotence had granted him the time. For his sake, God projected a secret miracle: German lead would kill him, at the determined hour, but in his mind a year would elapse between the command to fire and its execution. From perplexity he passed to stupor, from stupor to resignation, from resignation to sudden gratitude.

He disposed of no document but his own memory; the mastering of each hexameter, as he added it, had imposed upon him a kind of fortunate discipline not imagined by those amateurs who forget their vague, ephemeral paragraphs. He did not work for posterity, nor even for God, of whose literary preferences he possessed scant knowledge. Meticulous, unmoving, secretive, he wove his lofty invisible labyrinth in time. He worked the third act over twice. He eliminated some rather too-obvious symbols: the repeated striking of the hour, the music. There were no circumstances to constrain him. He omitted, condensed, amplified; occasionally, he chose the primitive version. He grew to love the courtyard, the barracks; one of the faces endlessly confronting him made him modify his conception of Roemerstadt's character. He discovered that the hard cacophonies which so distressed Flaubert are mere visual superstitions: debilities and annoyances of the written word, not of the sonorous, the sounding one. ... He brought his drama to a conclusion: he lacked only a single epithet. He found it: the drop of water slid down his cheek. He began a wild cry, moved his face aside. A quadruple blast brought him down.

Jaromir Hladík died on 29 March, at 9.02 in the morning.

1943   *Translated by* ANTHONY KERRIGAN

THREE VERSIONS OF JUDAS

> There seemed a certainty in degradation.
> T. E. Lawrence, *Seven Pillars of Wisdom*

In Asia Minor or in Alexandria, in the second century of our faith (when Basilides was announcing that the cosmos was a rash and malevolent improvisation engineered by defective angels), Nils Runeberg might have directed, with a singular intellectual passion, one of the Gnostic conventicles. Dante would have destined him, perhaps, for a fiery sepulchre; his name might have augmented the catalogues of heresiarchs, between Satornibus and Carpocrates; some fragment of his preaching, embellished with invective, might have been preserved in the apocryphal *Liber adversus omnes haereses* or might have perished when the firing of a monastic library consumed the last example of the *Syntagma*. Instead, God assigned him to the twentieth century, and to the university city of Lund. There, in 1904, he published the first edition of *Kristus och Judas*; there, in 1909, his masterpiece *Dem hemlige Fralsaren* appeared. (Of this last mentioned work there exists a German version, called *Der heimliche Heiland*, executed in 1912 by Emil Schering.)

Before undertaking an examination of the foregoing works, it is necessary to repeat that Nils Runeberg, a member of the National Evangelical Union, was deeply religious. In some salon in Paris, or even in Buenos Aires, a literary person might well rediscover Runeberg's theses; but these arguments, presented in such a setting, would seem like frivolous and idle exercises in irrelevance or blasphemy. To Runeberg they were the key with which to decipher a central mystery of theology; they were a matter of meditation and analysis, of historic and philologic controversy, of loftiness, of jubilation, and of terror. They justified, and destroyed, his life. Whoever peruses this essay should know that it states only Runeberg's conclusions, not his dialectic or his proof. Someone may

observe that no doubt the conclusion preceded the 'proofs'.
For who gives himself up to looking for proofs of something
he does not believe in or the prediction of which he does not
care about?

The first edition of *Kristus och Judas* bears the following
categorical epigraph, whose meaning, some years later, Nils
Runeberg himself would monstrously dilate: *Not one thing, but
everything tradition attributes to Judas Iscariot is false.* (De
Quincey, 1857.) Preceded in his speculation by some German
thinker, De Quincey opined that Judas had betrayed Jesus
Christ in order to force him to declare his divinity and thus
set off a vast rebellion against the yoke of Rome; Runeberg
offers a metaphysical vindication. Skilfully, he begins by
pointing out how superfluous was the act of Judas. He
observes (as did Robertson) that in order to identify a master
who daily preached in the synagogue and who performed
miracles before gatherings of thousands, the treachery of an
apostle is not necessary. This, nevertheless, occurred. To
suppose an error in Scripture is intolerable; no less intolerable
is it to admit that there was a single haphazard act in the most
precious drama in the history of the world. *Ergo*, the treachery
of Judas was not accidental; it was a predestined deed which
has its mysterious place in the economy of the Redemption.
Runeberg continues: The Word, when It was made flesh,
passed from ubiquity into space, from eternity into history,
from blessedness without limit to mutation and death; in
order to correspond to such a sacrifice it was necessary that a
man, as representative of all men, make a suitable sacrifice.
Judas Iscariot was that man. Judas, alone among the apostles,
intuited the secret divinity and the terrible purpose of Jesus.
The Word had lowered Himself to be mortal; Judas, the
disciple of the Word, could lower himself to the role of
informer (the worst transgression dishonour abides), and
welcome the fire which cannot be extinguished. The lower
order is a mirror of the superior order, the forms of the earth
correspond to the forms of the heavens; the stains on the skin
are a map of the incorruptible constellations; Judas in some
way reflects Jesus. Thus the thirty pieces of silver and the

kiss; thus deliberate self-destruction, in order to deserve damnation all the more. In this manner did Nils Runeberg elucidate the enigma of Judas.

The theologians of all the confessions refuted him. Lars Peter Engstrom accused him of ignoring, or of confining to the past, the hypostatic union of the Divine Trinity; Axel Borelius charged him with renewing the heresy of the Docetists, who denied the humanity of Jesus; the sharp-edged bishop of Lund denounced him for contradicting the third verse of chapter twenty-two of the Gospel of St Luke.

These various anathemas influenced Runeberg, who partially rewrote the disapproved book and modified his doctrine. He abandoned the terrain of theology to his adversaries and postulated oblique arguments of a moral order. He admitted that Jesus, 'who could count on the considerable resources which Omnipotence offers', did not need to make use of a man to redeem all men. Later, he refuted those who affirm that we know nothing of the inexplicable traitor; we know, he said, that he was one of the apostles, one of those chosen to announce the Kingdom of Heaven, to cure the sick, to cleanse the leprous, to resurrect the dead, and to cast out demons (Matthew 10: 7–9; Luke 9: 1). A man whom the Redeemer has thus distinguished deserves from us the best interpretations of his deeds. To impute his crime to cupidity (as some have done, citing John 12: 6) is to resign oneself to the most torpid motive force. Nils Runeberg proposes an opposite moving force: an extravagant and even limitless asceticism. The ascetic, for the greater glory of God, degrades and fortifies the flesh; Judas did the same with the spirit. He renounced honour, good, peace, the Kingdom of Heaven, as others, less heroically, renounced pleasure.* With a terrible lucidity he premeditated his offence.

In adultery, there is usually tenderness and self-sacrifice; in murder, courage; in profanation and blasphemy, a certain satanic splendour. Judas elected those offences unvisited by any virtues: abuse of confidence (John 12: 6) and informing.

* Borelius mockingly interrogates: *Why did he not renounce to renounce? Why not renounce renouncing?*

He laboured with gigantic humility; he thought himself unworthy to be good. Paul has written: *Whoever glorifieth himself, let him glorify himself in God* (I Corinthians 1: 31); Judas sought Hell because the felicity of the Lord sufficed him. He thought that happiness, like good, is a divine attribute and not to be usurped by men.*

Many have discovered *post factum* that in the justifiable beginnings of Runeberg lies his extravagant end and that *Dem hemlige Fralsaren* is a mere perversion or exacerbation of *Kristus och Judas*. Towards the end of 1907, Runeberg finished and revised the manuscript text; almost two years passed without his handing it to the printer. In October of 1909, the book appeared with a prologue (tepid to the point of being enigmatic) by the Danish Hebraist Erik Erfjord and bearing this perfidious epigraph: *In the world he was, and the world was made by him, and the world knew him not* (John 1: 10). The general argument is not complex, even if the conclusion is monstrous. God, argues Nils Runeberg, lowered himself to be a man for the redemption of the human race; it is reasonable to assume that the sacrifice offered by him was perfect, not invalidated or attenuated by omissions. To limit what he suffered to the agony of one afternoon on the cross is blasphemous.† To affirm that he was a man and that he was

---

* Euclydes da Cunha, in a book ignored by Runeberg, notes that for the heresiarch of Canudos, Antonio Conselheiro, virtue was 'a kind of impiety almost'. An Argentine reader could recall analogous passages in the work of Almafuerte. Runeberg published, in the symbolist sheet *Sju insegel*, an assiduously descriptive poem, 'The Secret Water': the first stanzas narrate the events of one tumultuous day; the last, the finding of a glacial pool; the poet suggests that the eternalness of this silent water checks our useless violence, and in some way allows and absolves it. The poem concludes in this way:

> *The water of the forest is still and felicitous,*
> *And we, we can be vicious and full of pain.*

† Maurice Abramowicz observes: 'Jésus, d'après ce scandinave, a toujours le beau rôle; ses déboires, grâce à la science des typographes, jouissent d'une réputation polyglotte; sa résidence de trente-trois ans parmis les humains ne fut, en somme, qu'une villégiature.' Erfjord, in the third appendix to the *Christelige Dogmatik*, refutes this passage. He writes that the crucifying of God has not ceased, for anything which has happened once in time is

incapable of sin contains a contradiction; the attributes of *impeccabilitas* and of *humanitas* are not compatible. Kemnitz admits that the Redeemer could feel fatigue, cold, confusion, hunger, and thirst; it is reasonable to admit that he could also sin and be damned. The famous text *He will sprout like a root in a dry soil; there is not good mien to him, nor beauty; despised of men and the least of them; a man of sorrow, and experienced in heartbreaks* (Isaiah 53: 2–3) is for many people a forecast of the Crucified in the hour of his death; for some (as, for instance, Hans Lassen Martensen), it is a refutation of the beauty which the vulgar consensus attributes to Christ; for Runeberg, it is a precise prophecy, not of one moment, but of all the atrocious future, in time and eternity, of the Word made flesh. God became a man completely, a man to the point of infamy, a man to the point of being reprehensible – all the way to the abyss. In order to save us, He could have chosen *any* of the destinies which together weave the uncertain web of history; He could have been Alexander, or Pythagoras, or Rurik, or Jesus; He chose an infamous destiny: He was Judas.

In vain did the bookstores of Stockholm and Lund offer this revelation. The incredulous considered it, a priori, an insipid and laborious theological game; the theologians disdained it. Runeberg intuited from this universal indifference an almost miraculous confirmation. God had commanded this indifference; God did not wish His terrible secret propagated in the world. Runeberg understood that the hour had not yet come. He sensed ancient and divine curses converging upon him; he remembered Elijah and Moses, who covered their faces on the mountain top so as not to see God; he remembered Isaiah, who prostrated himself when his eyes saw That One whose glory fills the earth; Saul, who was blinded on the road to Damascus; the rabbi Simon ben Azai, who saw Paradise and died; the famous soothsayer John of Viterbo,

repeated ceaselessly through all eternity. Judas, *now*, continues to receive the pieces of silver; he continues to hurl the pieces of silver in the temple; he continues to knot the hangman's noose on the field of blood. (Erfjord, to justify this affirmation, invokes the last chapter of the first volume of the *Vindication of Eternity*, by Jaromir Hladík.)

who went mad when he was able to see the Trinity; the Midrashim, abominating the impious who pronounce the *Shem Hamephorash*, the secret name of God. Wasn't he, perchance, guilty of this dark crime? Might not this be the blasphemy against the Spirit, the sin which will not be pardoned (Matthew 12: 3)? Valerius Soranus died for having revealed the occult name of Rome; what infinite punishment would be his for having discovered and divulged the terrible name of God?

Intoxicated with insomnia and with vertiginous dialectic, Nils Runeberg wandered through the streets of Malmö, praying aloud that he be given the grace to share Hell with the Redeemer.

He died of the rupture of an aneurysm, the first day of March 1912. The writers on heresy, the heresiologists, will no doubt remember him; he added to the concept of the Son, which seemed exhausted, the complexities of calamity and evil.

1944   *Translated by* ANTHONY KERRIGAN

THE END*

Lying prone, Recabarren half-opened his eyes and saw the slanting rattan ceiling. The thrumming of a guitar reached him from the other room; the invisible instrument was a kind of meagre labyrinth infinitely winding and unwinding. ... Little by little he returned to reality, to the daily details which now would never change. He gazed without sorrow at his great useless body, at the poncho of coarse wool wrapped around his legs. Outside, beyond the barred windows, stretched the plain and the afternoon. He had been sleeping, but the sky was still filled with light. Groping about with his left arm, he finally touched a bronze cowbell hanging at the foot of the cot. He banged on it two or three times; from the other side of the door the humble chords continued to reach him. The guitarist was a Negro who had shown up one night to display his pretensions as a singer: he had challenged another stranger to a drawn out contest of singing to guitar accompaniment. Bested, he nevertheless continued to haunt the general store, as if waiting for someone. He passed the hours playing on his guitar, but he no longer ventured to sing. Perhaps his defeat had embittered him. The other customers had grown accustomed to this inoffensive player. Recabarren, the shop-owner, would never forget the songs of the guitar contest: the next day, as he adjusted a load of maté upon a mule's back, his right side had suddenly died and he had lost his power of speech. By dint of taking pity on the misfortunes of the heroes of novels we come to take too much pity on our own misfortunes; not so the enduring Recabarren, who accepted his paralysis as he had previously accepted the rude

---

* This account of a knife fight with Martín Fierro, the Argentine gaucho of José Hernández' great folk poem, takes up the story of Fierro where the popular poem leaves off. A singing encounter, or challenge, with a black man (one of ten brothers, the eldest of whom has been killed) occurs towards the end of the poem. A fight is at that time averted. Borges here gives us the account of a subsequent meeting. (And see Prologue to *Artifices*.) – *Editor's note*.

solitude of America. Habituated to living in the present, like the animals, he gazed now at the sky and considered how the crimson circle around the moon presaged rain.

A boy with Indian features (one of his sons, perhaps) half-opened the door. Recabarren asked him with his eyes if there were anyone in the shop. The boy, taciturn, indicated by terse signs that there was no one. (The Negro, of course, did not count.) The prostrate man was left alone. One hand played briefly with the cowbell, as if he were wielding some power.

Beneath the final sun of the day, the plain seemed almost abstract, as if seen in a dream. A point shimmered on the horizon, and then grew until it became a horseman, who came, or seemed to come, towards the building. Recabarren saw the wide-brimmed hat, the long dark poncho, the dappled horse, but not the man's face; at length the rider tightened the reins and cut down the gallop, approaching at a trot. Some two hundred yards away, he turned sharply. Recabarren could no longer see him, but he heard him speak, dismount, tie the horse to the paling, and enter the shop with a firm step.

Without raising his eyes from his instrument, where he seemed to be searching for something, the Negro said gently:

'I was sure, *señor*, that I could count on you.'

The other man replied with a harsh voice:

'And I on you, coloured man. I made you wait a pack of days, but here I am.'

There was a silence. At length the Negro responded:

'I'm getting used to waiting. I've waited seven years.'

Without haste the other explained:

'I went longer than seven years without seeing my children. I saw them that day, but I didn't want to seem like a man always fighting.'

'I realize that. I understand what you say,' said the Negro. 'I trust you left them in good health.'

The stranger, who had taken a seat at the bar, laughed a deep laugh. He asked for a rum. He drank with relish, but did not drain it down.

'I gave them some good advice,' he declared. 'That's never

amiss, and it doesn't cost anything. I told them, among other things, that one man should not shed another man's blood.'

A slow chord preceded the Negro's reply:

'You did well. That way they won't be like us.'

'At least they won't be like me,' said the stranger. And then he added, as if he were ruminating aloud: 'Destiny has made me kill, and now, once more, it has put a knife in my hand.'

The Negro, as if he had not heard, observed:

'Autumn is making the days grow shorter.'

'The light that's left is enough for me,' replied the stranger, getting to his feet.

He stood in front of the Negro and said, with weariness:

'Leave off the guitar. Today there's another kind of counterpoint waiting for you.'

The two men walked towards the door. As he went out, the Negro murmured:

'Perhaps this time it will go as hard on me as the first time.'

The other answered seriously:

'It didn't go hard on you the first time. What happened was that you were anxious for the second try.'

They moved away from the houses for a good bit, walking together. One point on the plain was as good as another, and the moon was shining. Suddenly they looked at each other, halted, and the stranger began taking off his spurs. They already had their ponchos wound around their forearms when the Negro said:

'I want to ask you a favour before we tangle. I want you to put all your guts into this meeting, just as you did seven years ago, when you killed my brother.'

Perhaps for the first time in the dialogue, Martín Fierro heard the sound of hate. He felt his blood like a goad. They clashed, and the sharp-edged steel marked the Negro's face.

There is an hour of the afternoon when the plain is on the verge of saying something. It never says it, or perhaps it says it infinitely, or perhaps we do not understand it, or we understand it and it is as untranslatable as music. ... From his cot, Recabarren saw the end. A charge, and the Negro fell back; he lost his footing, feinted towards the other's face, and reached out in a great stab, which penetrated the stranger's chest. Then there was another stab, which the shop-owner did not clearly see, and Fierro did not get up. Immobile, the Negro seemed to watch over his enemy's labouring death agony. He wiped his bloodstained knife on the turf and walked back towards the knot of houses slowly, without looking back. His righteous task accomplished, he was nobody. More accurately, he became the stranger: he had no further mission on earth, but he had killed a man.

Translated by ANTHONY KERRIGAN

THE SECT OF THE PHOENIX

Those who write that the sect of the Phoenix originated in Heliopolis, and make it derive from the religious restoration which followed the death of the reformer Amenhotep IV, cite texts by Herodotus, Tacitus, and inscriptions from the Egyptian monuments; but they ignore, or try to ignore, the fact that the denomination of the sect by the name of Phoenix is not prior to Rabanus Maurus, and that the most ancient sources (the *Saturnalia*, or Flavius Josephus, let us say) speak only of the People of Custom or the People of the Secret. Gregorovius had already observed, in the Conventicles of Ferrara, that any mention of the Phoenix was extremely rare in oral language. In Geneva, I have spoken to artisans who did not understand me when I asked if they were men of the Phoenix, but who admitted, in the next breath, that they were men of the Secret. Unless I am mistaken, the same phenomenon is observable among the Buddhists: the name by which they are known to the world is not the same as the one they themselves pronounce.

Miklošić, in an overly famous page, has compared the sectarians of the Phoenix with the gipsies. In Chile and in Hungary there are sectarians of the Phoenix and there are also gipsies; beyond their ubiquity, they have very little in common. The gipsies are horsedealers, tinkers, smiths, and fortune tellers; the sectarians tend to practise the liberal professions successfully. The gipsies are of a certain definite physical type, and they speak – or used to speak – a secret language; the sectarians are indistinguishable from the rest of the world: the proof of it is that they have not suffered persecutions. Gipsies are picturesque and inspire bad poets. Narrative verse, coloured lithographs, and boleros pay no heed to the sectarians. ... Martin Buber declares that Jews are essentially pathetic; not all sectarians are, and some of them despise pathos; this public and notorious fact suffices to refute the vulgar error (absurdly defended by Urmann) which sees in the Phoenix a derivative of Israel. People think more or less as follows: Urmann was a sensitive man; Urmann was a Jew; Urmann associated with the sectarians in the ghetto at Prague; the affinity felt by Urmann serves to prove a fact. I cannot in good faith agree with this judgement. The fact that sectarians in a Jewish environment should resemble Jews does not prove anything; the undeniable fact is that they resemble, like Hazlitt's infinite Shakespeare, all the men in the world. They are everything to all men, like the Apostle. Only a short time ago Doctor Juan Francisco Amaro, of Paysandú, marvelled at the ease with which they became Spanish-Americans.

I have mentioned that the history of the sect does not record persecutions. Still, since there is no human group which does not include partisans of the Phoenix, it is also true that there has never been a persecution which they have not suffered or a reprisal they have not carried out. Their blood has been spilled, through the centuries, under opposing enemy flags, in the wars of the West and in the remote battles of Asia. It has availed them little to identify themselves with all the nations of the earth.

Lacking a sacred book to unify them as the Scripture does Israel, lacking a common memory, lacking that other social memory which is language, scattered across the face of the earth, differing in colour and features, only one thing – the Secret – unites them and will unite them until the end of time. Once upon a time, in addition to the Secret, there was a legend (and perhaps also a cosmogonic myth), but the superficial men of the Phoenix have forgotten it, and today they conserve only the obscure tradition of some cosmic punishment: of a punishment, or a pact, or a privilege, for the versions differ, and they scarcely hint at the verdict of a God who grants eternity to a race of men if they will only carry out a certain rite, generation after generation. I have compared the testimony of travellers, I have conversed with patriarchs and theologians; and I can testify that the performance of the rite is the only religious practice observed by the sectarians. The rite itself constitutes the Secret. And the Secret, as I have already indicated, is transmitted from generation to generation; but usage does not favour mothers teaching it to their sons, nor is it transmitted by priests. Initiation into the mystery is the task of individuals of the lowest order. A slave, a leper, a beggar plays the role of mystagogue. A child can indoctrinate another child. In itself the act is trivial, momentary, and does not require description. The necessary materials are cork, wax, or gum arabic. (In the liturgy there is mention of silt; this, too, is often used.) There are no temples specially dedicated to the celebration of this cult; a ruin, a cellar, an entrance way are considered propitious sites. The Secret is sacred, but it is also somewhat ridiculous. The practice of the mystery is furtive and even clandestine, and its adepts do not speak about it. There are no respectable words to describe it, but it is understood that all words refer to it, or better, that they inevitably allude to it, and thus, in dialogue with initiates, when I have prattled about anything at all, they have smiled enigmatically or taken offence, for they have felt that I touched upon the Secret. In Germanic literature there are poems written by sectarians, whose nominal theme is the sea, say, or the evening twilight; but they are, I can hear someone say, in some measure symbols of the Secret.

As stated by Du Cange in his Glossary, by way of apocryphal proverb, *Orbis terrarum est speculum Ludi*. A kind of sacred horror prevents some of the faithful from practising the extremely simple ritual; the others despise them for it, but they despise themselves even more. On the other hand, those sectarians who deliberately renounce the Custom and manage to engage in direct communication with the divinity enjoy a large measure of credit. To make this commerce manifest, these latter sectarians have recourse to figures from the liturgy; thus John of the Rood wrote:

> *May the Nine Firmaments know that God*
> *Is as delightful as cork or muck.*

I have enjoyed the friendship of devotees of the Phoenix on three continents; it seems clear to me that at first the Secret struck them as something paltry, distressing, vulgar and (what is even stranger) incredible. They could not reconcile themselves to the fact that their ancestors had lowered themselves to such conduct. The odd thing is that the Secret has not been lost long ago; despite the vicissitudes of the world, despite wars and exoduses, it extends, in its tremendous fashion, to all the faithful. One commentator has not hesitated to assert that it is already instinctive.

Translated by ANTHONY KERRIGAN

THE SOUTH

The man who landed in Buenos Aires in 1871 bore the name of Johannes Dahlmann and he was a minister in the Evangelical Church. In 1939, one of his grandchildren, Juan Dahlmann, was secretary of a municipal library on Calle Córdoba, and he considered himself profoundly Argentinian. His maternal grandfather had been that Francisco Flores, of the Second Line-Infantry Division, who had died on the frontier of Buenos Aires, run through with a lance by Indians from Catriel; in the discord inherent between his two lines of descent, Juan Dahlmann (perhaps driven to it by his Germanic blood) chose the line represented by his romantic ancestor of the romantic death. An old sword, a leather frame containing the daguerreotype of a blank-faced man with a beard, the dash and grace of certain music, the familiar strophes of *Martín Fierro*, the passing years, boredom and solitude, all went to foster this voluntary, but never ostentatious nationalism. At the cost of numerous small privations, Dahlmann had managed to save the empty shell of a ranch in the South which had belonged to the Flores family; he continually recalled the image of the balsamic eucalyptus trees and the great rose-coloured house which had once been crimson. His duties, perhaps even indolence, kept him in the city. Summer after summer he contented himself with the abstract idea of possession and with the certitude that his ranch was waiting for him on a precise site in the middle of the plain. Late in February, 1939, something happened to him.

Blind to all fault, destiny can be ruthless at one's slightest distraction. Dahlmann had succeeded in acquiring, on that very afternoon, an imperfect copy of Weil's edition of *The Thousand and One Nights*. Avid to examine this find, he did not wait for the elevator but hurried up the stairs. In the obscurity, something brushed by his forehead: a bat, a bird? On the face of the woman who opened the door to him he saw horror engraved, and the hand he wiped across his face came away red with blood. The edge of a recently painted door which someone had forgotten to close had caused this wound. Dahlmann was able to fall asleep, but from the moment he awoke at dawn the savour of all things was atrociously poignant. Fever wasted him and the pictures in *The Thousand and One Nights* served to illustrate nightmares. Friends and relatives paid him visits and, with exaggerated smiles, assured him that they thought he looked fine. Dahlmann listened to them with a kind of feeble stupor and he marvelled at their not knowing that he was in hell. A week, eight days passed, and they were like eight centuries. One afternoon, the usual doctor appeared, accompanied by a new doctor, and they carried him off to a sanatorium on Calle Ecuador, for it was necessary to X-ray him. Dahlmann, in the hackney coach which bore them away, thought that he would, at last, be able to sleep in a room different from his own. He felt happy and communicative. When he arrived at his destination, they undressed him, shaved his head, bound him with metal fastenings to a stretcher; they shone bright lights on him until he was blind and dizzy, auscultated him, and a masked man stuck a needle into his arm. He awoke with a feeling of nausea, covered with a bandage, in a cell with something of a well about it; in the days and nights which followed the operation he came to realize that he had merely been, up until then, in a suburb of hell. Ice in his mouth did not leave the least trace of freshness. During these days Dahlmann hated himself in minute detail: he hated his identity, his bodily necessities, his humiliation, the beard which bristled upon his face. He stoically endured the curative measures, which were painful, but when the surgeon told him he had been on the point of death from septicemia, Dahlmann dissolved in tears of self-pity for his fate. Physical wretchedness and the incessant anticipation of horrible nights had not allowed him time to think of anything so abstract as death. On another day, the surgeon told him he was healing and that, very soon, he would be able to go to his ranch for convalescence. Incredibly enough, the promised day arrived.

Reality favours symmetries and slight anachronisms:

Dahlmann had arrived at the sanatorium in a hackney coach and now a hackney coach was to take him to the Constitución station. The first fresh tang of autumn, after the summer's oppressiveness, seemed like a symbol in nature of his rescue and release from fever and death. The city, at seven in the morning, had not lost that air of an old house lent it by the night; the streets seemed like long vestibules, the plazas were like patios. Dahlmann recognized the city with joy on the edge of vertigo: a second before his eyes registered the phenomena themselves, he recalled the corners, the billboards, the modest variety of Buenos Aires. In the yellow light of the new day, all things returned to him.

Every Argentine knows that the South begins at the other side of Rivadavia. Dahlmann was in the habit of saying that this was no mere convention, that whoever crosses this street enters a more ancient and sterner world. From inside the carriage he sought out, among the new buildings, the iron grill windows, the brass knocker, the arched door, the entrance way, the intimate patio.

At the railroad station he noted that he still had thirty minutes. He quickly recalled that in a café on the Calle Brazil (a few dozen feet from Yrigoyen's house) there was an enormous cat which allowed itself to be caressed as if it were a disdainful divinity. He entered the café. There was the cat, asleep. He ordered a cup of coffee, slowly stirred the sugar, sipped it (this pleasure had been denied him in the clinic), and thought, as he smoothed the cat's black coat, that this contact was an illusion and that the two beings, man and cat, were as good as separated by a glass, for man lives in time, in succession, while the magical animal lives in the present, in the eternity of the instant.

Along the next to the last platform the train lay waiting. Dahlmann walked through the coaches until he found one almost empty. He arranged his baggage in the network rack. When the train started off, he took down his valise and extracted, after some hesitation, the first volume of *The Thousand and One Nights*. To travel with this book, which was so much a part of the history of his ill-fortune, was a kind of affirmation that his ill-fortune had been annulled; it was a joyous and secret defiance of the frustrated forces of evil.

Along both sides of the train the city dissipated into suburbs; this sight, and then a view of the gardens and villas, delayed the beginning of his reading. The truth was that Dahlmann read very little. The magnetized mountain and the genie who swore to kill his benefactor are – who would deny it? – marvellous, but not so much more than the morning itself and the mere fact of being. The joy of life distracted him from paying attention to Scheherazade and her superfluous miracles. Dahlmann closed his book and allowed himself to live.

Lunch – the bouillon served in shining metal bowls, as in the remote summers of childhood – was one more peaceful and rewarding delight.

Tomorrow I'll wake up at the ranch, he thought, and it was as if he was two men at a time: the man who travelled through the autumn day and across the geography of the fatherland, and the other one, locked up in a sanatorium and subject to methodical servitude. He saw unplastered brick houses, long and angled, timelessly watching the trains go by; he saw horsemen along the dirt roads; he saw gullies and lagoons and ranches; he saw great luminous clouds that resembled marble; and all these things were accidental, casual, like dreams of the plain. He also thought he recognized trees and crop fields; but he would not have been able to name them, for his actual knowledge of the countryside was quite inferior to his nostalgic and literary knowledge.

From time to time he slept, and his dreams were animated by the impetus of the train. The intolerable white sun of high noon had already become the yellow sun which precedes nightfall, and it would not be long before it would turn red. The railroad car was now also different; it was not the same as the one which had quit the station siding at Constitución; the plain and the hours had transfigured it. Outside, the moving shadow of the railroad car stretched towards the horizon. The elemental earth was not perturbed either by settlements or other signs of humanity. The country was vast but at the same

time intimate and, in some measure, secret. The limitless
country sometimes contained only a solitary bull. The solitude was perfect, perhaps hostile, and it might have occurred
to Dahlmann that he was travelling into the past and not
merely south. He was distracted from these considerations by
the railroad inspector who, on reading his ticket, advised him
that the train would not let him off at the regular station but
at another: an earlier stop, one scarcely known to Dahlmann.
(The man added an explanation which Dahlmann did not
attempt to understand, and which he hardly heard, for the
mechanism of events did not concern him.)

The train laboriously ground to a halt, practically in the
middle of the plain. The station lay on the other side of the
tracks; it was not much more than a siding and a shed. There
was no means of conveyance to be seen, but the station chief
supposed that the traveller might secure a vehicle from a
general store and inn to be found some ten or twelve blocks
away.

Dahlmann accepted the walk as a small adventure. The
sun had already disappeared from view but a final splendour
exalted the vivid and silent plain, before the night erased its
colour. Less to avoid fatigue than to draw out his enjoyment
of these sights, Dahlmann walked slowly, breathing in the
odour of clover with sumptuous joy.

The general store at one time had been painted a deep
scarlet, but the years had tempered this violent colour for its
own good. Something in its poor architecture recalled a steel
engraving, perhaps one from an old edition of *Paul et Virginie*.
A number of horses were hitched up to the paling. Once
inside, Dahlmann thought he recognized the shopkeeper.
Then he realized that he had been deceived by the man's
resemblance to one of the male nurses in the sanatorium.
When the shopkeeper heard Dahlmann's request, he said he
would have the shay made up. In order to add one more event
to that day and to kill time, Dahlmann decided to eat at the
general store.

Some country louts, to whom Dahlmann did not at first
pay any attention, were eating and drinking at one of the

tables. On the floor, and hanging on to the bar, squatted an old man, immobile as an object. His years had reduced and polished him as water does a stone or the generations of men do a sentence. He was dark, dried up, diminutive, and seemed outside time, situated in eternity. Dahlmann noted with satisfaction the kerchief, the thick poncho, the long *chiripá*, and the colt boots, and told himself, as he recalled futile discussions with people from the Northern counties or from the province of Entre Rios, that gauchos like this no longer existed outside the South.

Dahlmann sat down next to the window. The darkness began overcoming the plain, but the odour and sound of the earth penetrated the iron bars of the window. The shop owner brought him sardines, followed by some roast meat. Dahlmann washed the meal down with several glasses of red wine. Idling, he relished the tart savour of the wine, and let his gaze, now grown somewhat drowsy, wander over the shop. A kerosene lamp hung from a beam. There were three customers at the other table: two of them appeared to be farm workers; the third man, whose features hinted at Chinese blood, was drinking with his hat on. Of a sudden, Dahlmann felt something brush lightly against his face. Next to the heavy glass of turbid wine, upon one of the stripes in the table cloth, lay a spit ball of breadcrumb. That was all: but someone had thrown it there.

The men at the other table seemed totally cut off from him. Perplexed, Dahlmann decided that nothing had happened, and he opened the volume of *The Thousand and One Nights*, by way of suppressing reality. After a few moments another little ball landed on his table, and now the *peones* laughed outright. Dahlmann said to himself that he was not frightened, but he reasoned that it would be a major blunder if he, a convalescent, were to allow himself to be dragged by strangers into some chaotic quarrel. He determined to leave, and had already gotten to his feet when the owner came up and exhorted him in an alarmed voice:

'*Señor* Dahlmann, don't pay any attention to those lads; they're half high.'

Dahlmann was not surprised to learn that the other man, now, knew his name. But he felt that the conciliatory words served only to aggravate the situation. Previous to this moment, the *peones'* provocation was directed against an unknown face, against no one in particular, almost against no one at all. Now it was an attack against him, against his name, and his neighbours knew it. Dahlmann pushed the owner aside, confronted the *peones*, and demanded to know what they wanted of him.

The tough with a Chinese look staggered heavily to his feet. Almost in Juan Dahlmann's face he shouted insults, as if he had been a long way off. His game was to exaggerate his drunkenness, and this extravagance constituted a ferocious mockery. Between curses and obscenities, he threw a long knife into the air, followed it with his eyes, caught and juggled it, and challenged Dahlmann to a knife fight. The owner objected in a tremulous voice, pointing out that Dahlmann was unarmed. At this point, something unforeseeable occurred.

From a corner of the room, the old ecstatic gaucho – in whom Dahlmann saw a summary and cipher of the South (his South) – threw him a naked dagger, which landed at his feet. It was as if the South had resolved that Dahlmann should accept the duel. Dahlmann bent over to pick up the dagger, and felt two things. The first, that this almost instinctive act bound him to fight. The second, that the weapon, in his torpid hand, was no defence at all, but would merely serve to justify his murder. He had once played with a poniard, like all men, but his idea of fencing and knife-play did not go further than the notion that all strokes should be directed upwards, with the cutting edge held inwards. *They would not have allowed such things to happen to me in the sanatorium*, he thought.

'Let's get on our way,' said the other man.

They went out and if Dahlmann was without hope, he was also without fear. As he crossed the threshold, he felt that to die in a knife fight, under the open sky, and going forward to the attack, would have been a liberation, a joy, and a festive occasion, on the first night in the sanatorium, when they stuck

him with the needle. He felt that if he had been able to
choose, then, or to dream his death, this would have been the
death he would have chosen or dreamt.

Firmly clutching his knife, which he perhaps would not
know how to wield, Dahlmann went out into the plain.

Translated by ANTHONY KERRIGAN

ABOUT THE INTRODUCER

JOHN STURROCK has been a literary journalist since the mid-1960s. He has written books on the French New Novel, Borges, Structuralism, and autobiography; and has translated from both French and Spanish, including works by Alejo Carpentier, Hugo, Proust, and Stendhal.